Mother Rocket

MOTHER ROCKET

ROCKET

Stories by Rita Ciresi

The University of Georgia Press   Athens & London

Published by the University of Georgia Press
Athens, Georgia 30602

Designed by Sandra Strother Hudson
Set in Times Roman by Tseng Information Systems
Printed and bound by Thomson-Shore
The paper in this book meets the guidelines
for permanence and durability of the Committee on
Production Guidelines for Book Longevity
of the Council on Library Resources.

Printed in the United States of America
97 96 95 94 93 C 5 4 3 2 1

Library of Congress Cataloging in Publication Data

Ciresi, Rita.
Mother Rocket : stories / by Rita Ciresi.
p.   cm.
ISBN 0-8203-1508-7 (alk. paper)
PS3553.I7M68   1993
813'.54—dc20   92-22666
                                    CIP

British Library Cataloging in Publication Data available

For Jeff

and Celeste

Acknowledgments

Some of these stories first appeared in slightly different form in the following publications: "The Silent Partner" in *California Quarterly*, "Resurrection" in *Colorado Review*, "The End of the Season" in *Northern Review*, "Lifelines" in *South Carolina Review*, "Mother Rocket" in *Kingfisher*, and "Second Coming" in *Alaska Quarterly Review*.

I am grateful to the Pennsylvania Council on the Arts and the Pennsylvania State University for support to work on this project.

Contents

Mother Rocket

The Silent Partner

ntroducing his champion chatterbox, girlfriend Baby Bartholomew. Stuffed to the gills with jabber, she went bibbly babbly
all the blessed day. The only thing that surpassed her capacity
for speech was her amazing appetite for cookies. She ate them like a
squirrel, her cheeks puffed out, blithely spilling out the conversation
and trailing a line of crumbs behind her on the linoleum, attracting
every conceivable creeping, crawling insect. Where Baby went, so
went the ants. So went the noxious fumes of insecticide Tim was
forced to spray. It was chemical warfare all over again.

"Goddamn bugs," Tim grumped.

"Poor, disgusting little buggers," Baby said. "Kill 'em!"

Theirs was a tender romance. But the circumstances leading up to
it were drunken, noisy, and spectacular. It was the Gulf of Mexico
and the Fourth of July. Above them and before them, once in the air
and again in the mirror of the water, fireworks burst into color. Ooh,
went Baby. Baby went aah. She was somebody's kid sister, thirteen
years younger than Tim, and *into* this visual experience. What was
Tim into? He leaned down towards her as the M-8os thudded in the
distance. "Can't hear you," he said, giving him ample excuse to steer
her back to the silence of his place, where the conversation, guided by
the dopey effects of too many beers, got onto the subject of scars.

"I have got one helluva scar," Baby said, and rose, unsteady, from
her chair. Slowly, as if revealing her most camouflaged secret, she
pushed the hair off her forehead and exposed a barely visible white

thread cut into her hairline. She wasn't shy, either, about pulling that thread into a long, winding story, the gist of it being that at age five, while jump-roping, she tripped and fell onto a bottle cap, and was rushed to the hospital by her parents, and whisked off to an operating room by a nurse who was oh-so-kind to her, as was the Cuban doctor who couldn't spikka da English, but who patted her head and put three whole stitches in.

"Must have been traumatic, Baby."

"Oh, let me tell you, it was very, Tim."

That scar was her crowning glory. It was his inroad to Baby, and, in the ritual of seduction, his saving grace. Because of course she wanted to know if he had a scar, if he had many, and where, and why and WHAT! HE HAD SCARS ALL OVER? A question that brought a healthy pink blush to her fat little face, a blush that prompted Tim to coyly turn off the light.

But Baby's voice penetrated the mood he had tried to create. How could a girl check out a guy's scars in the dark? Was the point supposed to be that some scars were too deeply cut in to be revealed? Was the point supposed to be that some scars were meant to be felt and not seen?

"Yes, Baby. The last reason. That's the point."

Gotcha! In his arms, she had the mind of a historian. She begged to know the origin of each stripe that mapped his stomach, the holes that peppered his back. "Holy—well—whatever!" Baby exclaimed. He must have had a million operations. Tracheotomy, appendectomy, splenectomy. Stomach-ectomy? Lung-otomy? Baby was confused. Tim was excited. He was making love to her, but he was repeating "War, war, war!"

Baby gasped and pushed him away. "You mean you were in the real thing?"

"Is there a fake kind?"

"Well, I've heard there are some people—"

He grabbed her thick upper torso, white as a fish in the moonlight.

"—who get together and play—"

He thrust his tongue into her mouth to shut her up, his tongue working as a pacifier only as long as he could hold his breath. When he came up for air, she puffed, "—these crazy survival games—"

She struck Tim as incredible. She was a clean slate of naiveté. She was an overload of innocence he could never again cultivate within himself. She was always braced for a miracle, always seeking signs of faith. Always open to the penetration of a mystery, she dispelled the mystery by jabbering about it. She drove in the speed lane in a little red wagon. She shed her virginity, without mishap, on the lumpy mattress of a fold-out bed.

"I love your scars!" she whispered, at the point in the process when, technically, she was supposed to say *I love you*. But how she wished she had bled, bucketfuls, to lend some grandeur to this momentous event. She was just a teeny, just a teeny little bit disappointed, in herself, of course, but Tim, Tim, Tim! "What do you call this thingamajig?" she asked, and tapped on the tiny piece of plastic that plugged his left ear. The tap scratched through his body. "I've been wondering the whole time we were—well, *you know*—but I didn't dare ask if this is like another one of your war relics?"

Did she give him time to answer before moving on to the next volley of questions? No. She wanted to know did he get a Purple Heart for trading in his hearing? Did he hear amplified? In stereo? How much noise did he pick up with it?

"Sometimes," he said, "so much I wish I didn't have to hear at all."

He popped it out of his ear and handed it to her. She held it up in the moonlight, turning it this way and that in her hand. "It's cute," she said. "I really like it. I really like your little wiener, too. Does he have a name? Can I call him Roger? Would you like to hear a bedtime story about Roger Cock-a-doodle-doo?"

He'd pass on that one. Baby, undaunted, clasped his hearing aid and began another. "Don't tell me," she said. "All was quiet on the western front . . ."

According to her scenario, Tim had been crawling along in the mud and filth of a foxhole, sick of canned peaches, sick of canned Spam. Mosquitoes swarmed in the thick air; colorful birds, like, you know, the kind you saw on the Fruit Loops cereal box? sang dementedly. Tim had been thinking about Mom and Dad. He'd been thinking about ice cream and clean underwear and all the other things that represented the good old U.S. of A., when suddenly the enemy opened fire. Rat-a-tat-tat and rockets flying everywhere! His body tensed; his feet numbed. Then ka-bam! the enemy made a hit, knocking Tim smack off those numb feet—

"I thought I was crawling, Baby, on my belly, not my feet. And you need to put me in a real, honest-to-goodness trench, not some World War II foxhole."

"Do you want to hear this story or not?" Baby demanded. All right, then. All right. He had to give her free rein. Where were they? Oh yes, the enemy. That slitty-eyed crew of chopstick-users knocked Tim smack off those 10-ton combat boots of his. A loud boom thudded, and shocked the noise out of his left ear. He thought he might go totally deaf. He thought he might never hear the ringing of church bells, the voice of his high school sweetheart, or rock and roll, ever, ever again. He thought his ear canal was closed off forever, until one of his buddies leaned over and shouted, "YOU DEAD, TIMBO OLD BOY?"

Dead? Hell no. Alive. Alive, and he could still hear, blessed, blessed hear, if only in half instead of whole. He didn't even care if his stomach was split open, if three-quarters of his guts were spilling out, since he could listen to the whirl of the chopper as it carried him off to some heavenly hospital, thank God, and this was gospel according to Baby, more or less. Was she right?

Not quite. But he wasn't any Bible scholar of his own life, and if

Baby wanted to write her own apocrypha, so be it. He had just one question for her: did she go to the movies every weekend, or what?

Oh yes, for sure. For the air-conditioning and the candy and the popcorn and the way she thought she just might pee her pants from the excitement before the movie began. She just reveled in stories, and that probably explained why she sometimes talked a teeny bit much and apropos of that, shouldn't she stick this little thing back in his ear, so he could hear his loved one whispering and snoring all night long?

So this loved one snored? No kidding. He assured her he always left his hearing aid out. For there was nothing this good man liked more than a good night's sleep.

He intended it as a general hint for her to knock off the yakking. But there was no stifling the chirping of this tropical bird. She simply flew over to the side of his good ear and breathed that now that he had bared his body, he was obligated to bare his soul.

"It's bad manners, Baby, to spill your guts on the first date."

"First date? This is a sleepover!"

"Do you notice either one of us sleeping?"

"Did you sleep after losing your virginity?"

"No," he said. "I was standing up, in a barn in Minnesota in sub-zero weather. It seemed a more practical move to pull up my pants."

Oh, ho ho! Poor little Roger, hard as an icicle, frozen stiff. Tell her more, more.

Tim exhaled. Where was that blissful snoring she had just promised? He couldn't figure this baby out. She was like a cup of coffee drunk right before bedtime. She was worse. She made noise. Hadn't she read her Masters and Johnson? Didn't she realize that the average American male liked to do it and snooze and not stay up jawing all night about things that were over and done with?

—about his family, she was saying. About his childhood, about how old he was, about how old he felt, about his crib experience, his junior high experience, his love experience, his lack of love experience, his crucial sex experience, about whether he believed God was male or female, animal or vegetable, mineral or—

Nothing. He believed in nothing.

"What?" Baby shot up in bed, her breasts cockeyed in shock. "You don't believe in God?"

If there was a God, Tim reasoned, He, She, or It was indeed cruel and merciless for folding him, so sleepy, into the batter of this conversation. So there could be a God, yes sirree.

Baby leaned back down on her elbows and stared him wide-eyed in the face. "I love a man with doubts," she said. "I just want you to know that. It shows he has savoir faire. Been around. Seen the world. Known the score. Eaten his share of the pie."

His idea of savoir faire was putting away this piece of the pie for the moment and—

—talking about the future? Great! Baby loved the future. It was the land of dreams. It was the land in which Tim could be anything he wanted to be, so what would he be if the God he didn't believe in granted him another life? She'd be—

This was real trouble, when Baby started answering her own questions.

"—a puzzle," she said. "You know, the jigsaw kind. I'd be a picture of a log cabin, with gingham curtains in the windows and smoke coming out of the chimney. A water mill on the side, going round and round." She nudged him. "Well?"

He'd be a goddamn rocket, bursting into a million colors in fucking midair.

Too male. Decidedly too male for Baby. She just didn't understand the appeal of this fantasy of destruct and die. Deep inside, she was sure, every male rocket was a big male pussycat, meowing for his mama, licking his whiskers and seeking nothing but a little milk to drink.

"Let's get this straight, Baby. This man is not a pussycat man."

"Then tell mama what this un-pussycat man wants to be."

The digital clock clicked onto 2:30 A.M. He grabbed her arm and pinned it to the bed. "This man would like to be a man lying underneath a willow tree, with no one for miles around, sleeping, sleeping, sleeping very peacefully."

"But there'd be a picnic basket . . ." She caught up his thread. "With wine and a feast of food to spread out. Ham and chicken and potato salad and cookies, mounds of cookies, Oreos and shortbread biscuits, cream pies and Mallomars, oatmeals and chocolate chips." Mmm. Made her sleepy just thinking about it.

Tim clapped his hand on his stomach to suppress its growl. Baby yawned, drew the sheet over them both, and curled up next to him. "I don't sleep with the sheet," Tim felt like protesting. "And it's too hot to lie so close. Keep your distance. Move away." She was all downy warmth, a little stuffed animal, a silly goose, a feathered duck who had quacked herself straight to sleep. If only he could quack himself off into the land of dreams, too. But it was impossible. She slept with her mouth open, her steady breathing only serving to measure the quiet that now engulfed him. So this was what they meant by the phrase *The silence was deafening. . . .*

She slept like a corpse beneath that unbloodied white shroud. He got up, got dressed, and slipped out of the apartment. The steamy night air fertilized his appetite. He had his mind on that imaginary picnic basket. He had his mind on pepperoni pizza, on olives and peppers and his fair share of anchovies on top. So she was stuffed to the gills with jabber? Goddamn if he was going to bring her back a piece.

Baby grew on him, like mold in the bathtub, fungus on kitchen tile. He got used to her jawing. Pity it drowned out the hum of the natural world singing, the palms rustling, the sharp pitch of the crickets, the downpour of rain that monsooned them every evening, but what joy it washed out the sound of suicide, whispering insidiously within his head. All his life he had listened to the strains of destruction. Now it was time to listen to Baby, happily clucking as she built them a little nest.

They moved into a green stucco house. The green house, unlike much of anything in that coastal town, had a history. "It used to be the county hospital, would you get a load of that?" said Carla, the house super, as they signed the lease. That had been at the turn of the century, when the county had been more jungle than development, more overgrown with palms and melaluccas and banyan trees than with the multistoried condominiums that now marked the landscape. Baby just couldn't shut up about it. To think that the halls of the green house, wide enough to oblige bicycle and boxes, the occasional old mattress, the dilapidated chair, once had accommodated stretchers and wheelchairs and hospital beds. Couldn't Tim just hear the clank of iron upon the linoleum? And to think that the large walk-in closets that stood at the end of each hall, each now containing filthy metal garbage cans blossoming with colonies of the very insects Tim had so set his mind upon exterminating, once had been stacked high with row upon row of fresh white linens. Who had washed them? Ironed them? Tim shut off his hearing aid just as Baby began to reconstruct, body by body, the shades of the ghosts who had folded the sheets in the green house's hallway.

That house had a million doors. Every room had an entrance onto the hallway, and every room had a now-defunct buzzer call button that gave occasion to Baby's favorite game. Tim and Baby ate and ate and ate. After they chowed down too many tacos and enchiladas for dinner, and washed it all down with so much beer that when they stood up from the table they actually heard the contents of their stomachs sloshing, one or the other of them—it didn't matter who—would press the call button and pretend to ring the doctor for help. Baby chanted the

same jump-rope song she'd sung when she was small, the song that
had led to her most major surgery:

> IN *came the doctor*
> IN *came the nurse*
> IN *came the lady with the alligator purse!*

Then they rushed into each other's arms, and donning imaginary
stethoscopes, they checked each other's vital signs, giggling as they
pronounced each other guilty of overeating. Rx for gluttony: an after-
dinner tumble in the overheated front room, the box fan slicing the
sunset into a million slivers of light on the walls and ceiling. It was
a fun game. Baby was always up for a laugh. But sometimes Tim
felt overwhelmed by a wave of sadness. Maybe it was the getting up
afterwards that got to him, the washing of the dirty dishes to prevent a
fresh burgeoning of the insect population. Maybe it was the persistent
whisperings of Baby, who couldn't plug her mouth even when he was
plugging it, to the best of his ability, straight on into her. That chatter!
When she wasn't talking she was belly dancing, in body language that
shouted downright dirty. "You should learn how to do this," she said,
bumping and gyrating her way around the apartment, Mata Hari to his
Sheik of Araby.

"Could you not do that?" he asked. "It reminds me of whores."

"But there's nothing more madonnalike." She thrust forward her
pelvis. "It's great training for natural childbirth."

"I don't want to have kids."

"And it's a great way to work off my cookies."

"You eat enough of them."

"You're an insect. With big, droopy bags under his bug eyes."

Bug-eyed was right. He'd never had trouble sleeping before that
eternal summer. He lay in bed, not hot enough to sweat but stagnant
enough to feel sticky and uncomfortable, listening to the whir of the

fan and the click of the digital clock beside the bed. Baby, his dream out loud, slept on, while he wasn't even blessed with a nightmare. Countless nights he rose and crept into the kitchen. When he opened the refrigerator, casting on to the floor the beam of the interior light, the thin shadows of insects scurried across the tile. He slugged down half a quart of milk straight from the carton. He thought about the many times he'd been in the hospital, when morphine, at least, had numbed the tom-tom drum of his own mortality beating inside his head. What would numb him now? The tomato rotting on the plate on the refrigerator's second shelf? The empty jelly jar neither he nor Baby had ever gotten around to throwing out? Where was God when you stared into an empty refrigerator late at night?

He was hiding in the golden barrel of Plochmann's mustard. And inside the cabinet under the sink, all the potatoes were growing fluorescent eyes.

This was the silence of the night, crazy, stifled dumbness. It was so solemn, so funereal, it made Tim gag. It was killing him, until next door, Sly and Esperanza moved in. Carla had given him the skeleton dope on that couple, and Tim, who had long ago succumbed to Baby's faith in imagination, had filled the rest in. Esperanza waitressed the breakfast shift at Bill's Luncheonette. Her lush and fleshy body, made more curvaceous by the tightness of her uniform, left the green house at the crack of dawn. As she scooped dimes and quarters off Bill's counter, she burst out of her black apron like a ripe mango split open its skin as it rotted in the sun. Sly was another matter. He was a pushy customer. Maybe he'd met Esperanza at Bill's over a side order of grits and buckwheat pancakes. Sly wanted his eggs scrambled and Esperanza brought them out fried. He wanted black coffee and she brought it in with cream. He wanted white toast, and she brought out wheat. In honor of all this luscious movement, maybe he left her a hefty tip. Maybe he left her a dirty message written on the napkin he never bothered to put in his lap. *You should serve yourself sunny-side up. How about a little bacon makin'? Honey, Sly would like to squirt all over you!*

He probably was stamped in green all over his body. He had tattoos. They said ESPERANZA. They said MAMA. They said CHARLIE COMPANY. They said FLORIDA, LOVE IT OR LEAVE IT. They said, straight across the crack of his ass, DON'T TREAD ON ME.

They proclaimed Sly's superiority. They said this was the body that, persistent as the noonday sun, predictable as the five o'clock rain, would return home to the green house every night at 2 A.M. (maybe he was a cook; maybe a bartender) and wake Esperanza into action. Tim buried his head in the pillow when he heard Sly's boots squeak by in the hallway.

Then he started listening.

Carla lived beneath Esperanza and Sly. "Man," she said, "those two are heavy-duty fuckers. They make my ceiling shake. They make the blades of my fan go round and round. They're gonna save me a few cents come electric bill time."

He heard them without his hearing aid. He heard them in his dreams. He slept fitfully through their lovemaking. Baby slept oblivious to it all, until the night Sly pushed Esperanza against their wall (her weight hitting against it with a thud) and gave it to her, repeating, "Leeen-da, leeen-da, leeen-da."

Linda was Baby's real name.

"Tim," she shook him, "someone is calling me."

Tim feigned sleep.

"Someone is calling me," Baby said again.

"That's just Sly, Baby."

"Who? What?" Sensing a story, her eyes lit up in the moonlight.

He resented her intrusion into his own imaginary scenario. Sly and Esperanza were none of Baby's business. "It's not you Sly wants. It's Esperanza. He's calling her *linda*, beautiful, in Spanish."

Oh? Tim knew Spanish? She didn't know he knew Spanish. Funny how you could live with someone for a couple of months and not even know something major like their knowing Spanish, and where'd he learn Spanish anyway?

"Philippines."

Philippines! She didn't know he'd been to the Philippines. What was he doing in the Philippines? Funny how you could live with someone for practically two months and not even know they'd been to the Philippines, and where were the Philippines anyway?

Sly orgasmed. Tim shook with anger. "Baby, Baby, Baby, shut up!"

Then there was silence, the kind that followed the rumble of an earthquake, the soft, still calm in the eye of the storm. Esperanza's final moans punctuated Baby's strange, strangled weeping.

She really had just wanted to know him! She wanted to create the many chunks of him that seemed absent, incomprehensible, missing. She wanted to know what he was like when he was small. Had he ever jump-roped? Swung on swings? Had a tree house? Killed birds with slingshots? Played cowboys and Indians? What costumes had he worn on Halloween? Was he allowed to cut jack-o-lanterns or did he have to settle for drawing evil faces on his pumpkins with a Magic Marker?

"I'm not your puzzle, Baby."

No. He never would be with such a vital piece missing.

That being—?

His heart.

Heartless, he told her to imagine it.

> *First comes love, then comes marriage,*
> *Then comes another Baby in the baby carriage!*

Tim bolted up in bed. In the bathtub, Baby splashed and sang the little song he prayed was not a prophecy. He tried to remember if, the night before, he had proposed to her. He tried to remember when she had her last period. He held his head in his hands. Everything was cloudy. He was blurry-eyed after only two or three hours of what he could not legitimately call sleep. He had tossed and turned after Sly and Esperanza went silent, and right before he awoke he dreamed that he had strangled Baby, her thick neck cracking in his bare hands. With a little mouth-to-mouth, he tried to revive her. He tickled her. He poured cold water on her face. Then, disgusted at his inability to play Jesus to her Lazarus, he left her limp body on the linoleum and permanently killed her off by spraying her with a heavy dose of Raid. Baby, unlike a cockroach, didn't flail her legs and try to escape. She just died.

"Three blind mice!" Baby sang. "Three blind mice!" Tim held his ears. The whole world suddenly seemed too loud to hear. It was a world for talkers, for laughers, for music makers, for baby girls dancing the cha-cha as they wiggled their broad butts into too-tight cotton underpants. It was not a world for those who liked to keep quiet, for those who were incapable of supporting the sounds that reverberated inside their own heads. Tim lay down and rolled over on his good ear. He rolled back when Baby, hair frizzed and skin strapped pink from her hot bath, pinched him on the arm.

"I said, don't you feel good? Aren't you going to work?"

It struck Tim that this was the first adult thing he had ever heard Baby say. He shook his head. The idea of setting shingles on a hot tar roof all day made him shudder. "I feel funny," he told Baby.

"Funny-bunny?" she asked, and hefted her squat body back into bed next to him, Baby once again. "Got the sniffles? Got the flu bug? Got the shivers and the shakes, the hots and colds, the little achey pains of fever they talk about on TV?"

He saw Baby quickly warming up to the prospect of staying home with him, Florence Nightingale to his dying soldier, bustling about efficiently with cold washcloths and a rectal thermometer, administering alcohol rubs and hot chicken soup transfusions. She hated her job, standing behind the food counter of a department store, even though every now and then she got to snitch candy from the glass case. "Just think," she whispered to Tim, as if she were on the FBI's most wanted list, "I could get arrested for shoplifting just for eating one bite of Russell Stover licorice!"

He preferred the idea of her getting thrown in jail to the idea of her staying home with him and talking about it. Let her stuff her jaws with chocolate, while he lay peaceful in the jaws of death.

"I'll be all right. Go to work now."

Baby's chubby lower lip drooped with disappointment. She solemnly gave him a pouty, tender kiss, as if it were a drug that would save his life. She sang her baby-nonsense as she stuffed her chubby thighs into her pantyhose. "Timmy has a tummy, his tummy has an ache." By the time Baby got out the door, she had sung all about his headaches, neckaches, backaches, armaches, elbowaches, and forgetting about the conversation they had the night before, she endowed him with a heart and extolled his heartaches. "Bye-bye, sweetie-puss." She kissed him. "Baby-waby loves you. Keep your ear peeled for Sly and Esperanza."

Tim did. He spent the morning in bed, but he heard nothing but the hum of the box fan. In the afternoon he popped in his hearing aid, flattened a few cockroaches with one of Baby's high-heeled shoes, and went down to sit on the front porch. He smoked cigarettes and stared at the back of his knuckles, until Carla pulled up to the porch, her thin bottom cracked on the saddle of a rickety blue bike.

As she bent over the mailbox, her hard little breasts poked through her too-tight terry playsuit. "Laid off?" she asked.

"Excuse me?"

"You lose your job?" she said, louder this time.

He shook his head. "I don't feel good."

Too much cigarette smoke and sun had thinned Carla's eyes into a permanent squint. "You look all right to me." Her voice was throaty, slut-husky. "Check this out. Gimme a cigarette." She traded a magazine, in a brown paper wrapper, for one of Tim's Winstons. Tim tore off the wrapper and spread out the centerfold. Carla peered over his shoulder. She whistled. "Black and white in color. Whoo-eee."

A naked white woman, on all fours and bound in chains, extended her tongue towards a black woman with spread legs. Another white woman sat on the black woman's face, while a black man, kneeling, held the first white woman by the chains as he stuck it to her from behind.

Tim flipped through the magazine and found more of the same.

"You like that, don't you?" Carla asked.

"It's all right."

Carla lit her Winston and hopped up onto the porch rail, her shoulders hunched over and her chest as sunken as if she had lost a lung to emphysema. Tim stared at her toenails, encrusted with the last vestiges of a long-ago coat of red polish, the big toenail of her right foot unpainted, but ringed with yellow fungus and blackened by a bruise underneath.

"You hear Sly and Company last night?" she asked.

Tim nodded.

"All that screaming and screwing?"

Tim nodded again.

"You like those two?"

Tim shrugged. "They're all right."

Carla laughed and pulled her stringy brown hair into a ponytail. "You're a real talkative guy."

"So they tell me."

"Guess you let your girlfriend do the talking for you."

"Talking *at* me," Tim corrected her.

"That's the whole world," Carla said. "There's talkers, and then there's listeners. You a listener?"

Tim started to nod, but then, out of stubbornness, shook his head.

Carla blew smoke rings. "I meet a lot of guys," she said. "And every guy is just like a snowflake, different from all the rest. So what kind of snowflake are you?"

Tim shrugged.

"You got a past?" Carla asked.

"Doesn't everybody?"

Carla looked him up and down. "You in the war? That's what your baby-girl girlfriend told me." Carla raised her voice into a childish squeak. " 'He knows how to shoot a gun and he's even been to the Philippines. I don't even know where the Philippines are.' "

Tim winced to hear Baby so well parodied.

"You ever kill anybody, soldier?"

Tim squinted at her. "What do you think?"

Carla squinted back. "I think you killed plenty."

"I think you think right, then."

Carla smiled a slow smile. With half-shut eyes, she gazed down at her skinned knees. "My ex was a vet," she said. "A marine, man. Crazy fucker. Kept me up all night with his bad dreams. When he didn't have bad dreams, he had insomnia, and he'd spend all night on the phone with his buddies in Honolulu. Man, for what those calls cost we coulda lived in Hawaii, dancing in grass skirts and swilling the mai-tais. That'd be the life."

Tim nodded.

"But this was the real life, man," Carla said. "He was nuts and we were poor and one night he can't get through to Hawaii. It's three in the morning and I'm sleeping pretty peaceful, when all of a sudden I heard this wild Tarzan call coming out of nowhere. I figure the ex has killed a mega-cockroach or something, maybe even cornered a rat, so I open my eyes, and in the other room I see him hanging by his hands from the ceiling fan, yelling this crazy stuff about how the blades remind him of choppers and choppers remind him of death and death reminds him of dying. 'I can't take it anymore!' he yells. 'I can't take it!' Well, I wasn't taking any of that. I'm hopping mad he woke me up in the middle of the night. 'Get offa my ceiling fan!' I yell at him. Because it was the expensive kind, you know? with the gold on the blades and the Tiffany lamp in the center. 'Get offa my fan,' I yell, 'you crazy motherfucker!' But it was too late. He weighed 190 to start, and he had on his combat boots, which jacked him up another ten or fifteen. Down came my fan. Ripped it right outta the ceiling, and he's lying there like an idiot with Tiffany glass and gold slivers all around him. 'You crazy fucker,' I said, 'why don't you go back where you belong, in the crazy, fucking jungle!' So he takes off and I never see the crazy fucker again." Carla stared intently at Tim. She laughed. "You like that story?"

Tim shrugged. "It was all right."

Carla jutted out her chin. "You like that magazine, why don't you keep it?"

Tim looked down at the magazine. He could take it or leave it. "All right."

"Show it to your girlfriend," Carla suggested.

Tim shuffled through the pages, imagining Baby's giggly, shocked reaction. "She wouldn't like it."

"What does she like?"

Tim looked up.

"I said, soldier, what does she like?"

Carla looked him hard in the face. Tim swallowed, then shrugged. "The usual thing."

"You like the usual thing, too?"

Tim nodded. "The usual thing is all right."

Carla's apartment was a made-for-TV bordello—red velvet couch, leopard-skin rug, gold fringe dangling from the lampshades. Her bedroom was littered with empty cigarette packs and foil gum wrappers.

"Strip," she said, and Tim did.

She walked around him, like a drill sergeant inspecting him on parade. She let out a low whistle. "Your body's been through hell.

Your body's been through World War III." Tim grew hard as she circled around him. She poked Roger. "At ease, soldier."

Roger, ever the defiant military man, refused to obey.

Carla popped open the snaps of her playsuit. She wore no underwear. Her skinny body was brown and dirty; her sheets, under Tim's skin, were stiff and cruddy.

"You know this used to be a hospital," she said, scratching a nipple. "This used to be the emergency room. Where you live, they used to do operations. Our friends Sly and Esperanza, they live in the morgue." She climbed onto the bed. "What can the doctor do for you today? A little oral surgery?" The sweet little sucking of Baby became, with Carla, a hard lapping sound that made him ache. "You hear me eating you off, you deaf GI?" Carla gripped his thighs. "You like it this way, soldier? You like it like that?"

It was the 1700s. Maybe it was the 1600s; under the ether of sleep, Tim's sense of history reeled. He was a Spanish soldier, trudging behind De Soto—or was it Ponce de Leon?—in search of the fountain of youth. His skin was burnt red; his feet were muddy; he was crashing through the undergrowth with a machete. The sun blinded him. He made his way into a clearing. There, in glowing splendor, posed a statue of Youth, in the fat little form of Baby. She held a bow in her hand. She raised the bow and shot an arrow, sharp as love, into his heart. He fell to the ground, wounded. He was bitten by a snake. He was chewed half to death by mosquitoes. *Ayuda, ayudame,* he moaned. Then he was in a helicopter; Carla drove. Back at the green house, Esperanza shot his butt up with anesthesia, while Sly, that crusty old doctor, sharpened the knife. Tim flinched, clutched his balls, and woke up.

Carla was AWOL. He was stretched flat on her bed, sweating to the whir of the ceiling fan. He grabbed his pants off the floor. There was nothing that made him feel so hollow, so useless, as pulling on his trousers, leg after leg, after lovemaking. He went back upstairs and collapsed, once again, on the bed.

"Naughty boy!" Baby said later, when she came home. "Naughty, naughty boy! You slept through the fireworks. I know. Carla told me." Tim heard Carla's name and Carla's name alone. "Carla. Oh God. Kill me."

"Kill you?" Baby climbed on top of Tim and straddled him. "Why should I kill you? I just wondered why you hadn't woken up. Carla said . . ." Here Baby slit her eyes and lowered her voice, imitating Carla as perfectly as Carla had mimicked her before. " 'I think that soldier of yours has already seen his share of the action.' "

"All right. Kill me. Shoot me, Baby, fast and quick."

"Shoot you?" Baby looked quizzical, as if she had just pronounced the first word of her life and had absolutely no idea what it meant. Then her eyes lit up as she envisioned the scenario, the crack of the firearm, Tim tumbling to the floor, the gun smoking in her hand as the police stormed the entrance. "Baby Bartholomew?" the chief of police asked. "*The* Baby Bartholomew, champion yakker, thief of Russell Stover licorice, Florida's most wanted mankiller? Okay boys, book her. Lock her up."

And throw away the key. Tim's mother, long ago, had pretended to lock up his mouth when she wanted peace and quiet, and then she went through the motion of throwing the imaginary key in the waste-basket. It had worked. Tim kept quiet. Maybe that was why he was so silent, because his mother had died of pneumonia before she could retrieve the key and unlock him. His father was all locked up too, in that rural Minnesota fashion, where you never said anything unless somebody said something to you first . . .

"—so exciting!" Baby was saying. Her eyes rolled with the delirium of it. "I called the police. The police told Carla to stay in her apart-ment. I'm a witness. A photographer took a picture of me. There's going to be the death penalty—"

The death penalty? For Carla or for Tim? For giving head or suck-ing pussy? Police, photographers, all that for just a few minutes of harmless pleasure?

"Baby, you're overreacting," Tim said.

"Overreacting? To a murder?"

"Murder?"

Baby, goo-goo-eyed, tapped Tim on the hearing aid. "Aren't you listening? It's Sly. Who killed Esperanza. Esperanza's dead!"

It was Baby who first smelled it, on her way past their door after work. "It stunk like something in the middle of the road," she said. "A skunk or maybe a dead possum, rotten alligator meat maybe. So I went down and knocked on Carla's door." Carla—oh my God!— her mouth was all drunk and her eyes all squinty and she answered the door in—Baby giggled—a red G-string that said on the strap *This Florida Native Still Burns!* Hee, hee, hee! The words were stitched in gold and the crotch was clotted up with—well, Tim could just imagine—some man's disgusting old dried-up come! Baby chortled. It was disgusting. But she tried not to laugh. "Excuse me for bothering you, Carla," she said, "but I smell something just a little bit pee-u upstairs." Carla was drunk and didn't make any sense. "Don't blame me for the smell of your own shit," she said. Shit? Baby was confused and amused. Carla was like a drunk old wino on a park bench, her body so skinny and ugly and dirty she looked like she could use a month's stay at the Salvation Army. Baby had never seen such an ugly, skinny, dirty body in her life. She wondered how Carla ever got a date on Friday night. Tim should check it out next time he saw her.

Tim swallowed. Would Baby please get on with the story?

All right. All right. So Baby told Carla, "There's something just a little bit pee-u coming out of Sly and Esperanza's apartment," and hee, hee, hee, Carla started to walk upstairs in her G-string until Baby called her back and told her she might want to put something on. "Right," Carla mumbled, and then she put on this black lace negligee, as if that hid anything. Carla marched upstairs, took one whiff, and pounded the palm of her hand on Sly and Esperanza's door. "All right, you crazy Cuban motherfuckers, open this fucking door!" The smell was like—well, what was the word? Odoriferous? Carla said, "Smells like a dead fucker in there to me. Call your boyfriend, Baby, and we'll bust down this door."

"He's asleep," Baby said. "I'll wake him up."

"Don't bother. I guess that soldier of yours has seen his share of the action today."

They went downstairs, and from Carla's apartment Baby called the cops. "Officer, I'd like to report a murder!" Baby cried to the bored dispatcher on the other end of the line.

"Did you commit this murder, ma'am?" the dispatcher asked.

"No sir, but I smell it, and I smell it good."

Well. They thought she was a crazy lady, so they took their sweet time a-moseying over. Then Carla—Baby screeched—Carla actually answered the door in that negligee and G-string of hers. The policemen didn't bat an eye. "You report a murder, ma'am?" one of them asked, at which point Baby took over, spilled the whole story, about Sly and Esperanza and Sly's tattoos and Esperanza's painful, wonderful moaning, until the officer took her by the hand and pulled her upstairs, telling Carla, "I think you better stay here, ma'am."

Carla put her hand on her hip and stuck out her skinny ass. "Don't you worry. I was thinking about doing just that."

The policemen jingled like Christmas bells as they went up the stairs. They had keys and whistles and all sorts of handcuffs and if Tim weren't so deaf he would have awakened at the sound of all that jingling. They had guns. They had billy clubs. They had badges—

Would Baby please just make this long story short?

All right! Baby glared at Tim. The policemen broke down the door. They found Esperanza slumped over on the floor, naked and swollen like a frog, covered with more bruises than Tim had scars. End of story.

Baby climbed off Tim, lifted the skirt of her dress, and peeled off her pantyhose. Tim watched. Even Baby's knees were chubby, the fat, padded little joints of a newborn baby. Knees. He shook his head. Why was he thinking about those senseless parts of the human body when on the other side of the wall, just an hour ago, lay somebody dead? Was this the point of waking up in the middle of the night, to be a silent accessory to someone's murder? He heard her cry out. *Ayuda, ayudame!* He had heard her moan and gasp, and thought she was in the grip of love, when really she had been dying.

Baby turned against the breeze of the box fan and her dress plastered against her body. "I'd like to have a baby, someday," she said. "A baby would listen to my stories."

And one of them would go like this: Once there was a boy named Tim. Once there was a girl nicknamed—hee, hee!—Baby. Tim was grim. Baby was silly. Tim grew up in the cold, cold tundra of a stupid old place called Minnesota. Outside his house lay drifts of snow so high Tim could sled down to the barn from his second-story bedroom window. He ate icicles every night instead of his supper. He was a cold, cold boy. He was a snow boy, an ice boy, and nobody, not even his farmer father or his nice sweet mommy, who made him gingerbread cookies and apple pie, could warm that boy up.

Poor boy. His mommy got pneumonia. That's when your lungs get all clogged up with mucus and you can't breathe and then you die. His daddy only said, "Your mother's dead" and nothing more, so Timmy-Tim-Tim took a gun into the barn and popped pigeons off the rafters just to hear something talking. The guns chattered pellets, and the pigeons cooed before they went plop! into the hay. Timmy didn't like his daddy much, so when he grew up he went into the army.

Timmy went to Singapore. Timmy went to Germany. Timmy went to the Philippines, which are these teeny, tiny little old islands in the middle of the Pacific Ocean. Timmy went to Indonesia. Timmy went to Vietnam. Timmy killed lots and lots of people, but mostly he just sat around in the hot old sun, waiting to die like his mommy did, and his daddy did, years later. Somewhere along the line Timmy lost the hearing in his funny little ear. He had to go home to America and find something else to do besides kill people and wait to die, so he moved to Florida and put lots of shingles on lots of people's roofs, but really he still existed to kill and maybe to commit suicide. He liked to kill these sometimes teeny, sometimes gigantic bugs called cockroaches. He kept his ear peeled for a call from God, but he made himself even more deaf listening to the fan whirring in the window and the hum of the refrigerator and the awful, awful sound of nothing.

Years and years go by. Millions of bugs are laid to waste. Tim lays lots of girls. He lays lots of shingles. Then he meets a nice little girl, the Baby girl mentioned before. Oh, he makes Baby oh so happy! He kisses her and pets her. He bites her little boobies and tickles her (tee, hee, hee!). They are the perfect couple. God must have made them just for one another. Baby likes to talk lots and Timmy likes to listen.

They move into an old hospital converted into an apartment building. Baby nurses Timmy and Timmy doctors Baby. They meet a skinny girl named Carla who is not so nice. Next door live two mysterious Cubans who make a lot of noise, so much noise that poor Timmy can't get to sleep. He gets bug-eyed. He gets just a little bit crazy when one night he overhears the nice Cuban lady die. Baby finds the body and tells him all about it. Baby likes excitement, but gets mad when Tim won't listen. "I'd like to have a baby someday," she tells Tim. "A baby would listen to my story."

And it would go like this: Baby, Baby, stick your head in gravy, you're more grim than your boyfriend Timmy. Timmy—hee, hee— does a naughty thing to Baby. Baby takes off her pantyhose and says she wants a baby. Timmy wants to give her a baby the way all daddy-boys do, but, you see, he's done a very, very bad thing with the evil, skinny old girl named Carla that afternoon, and when he tries to give Baby her baby he gives her a very, very bad disease instead. Oh, oh, oh! Soon Baby feels funny. She feels sort of feverish, sort of dizzy. She thinks maybe she really is going to have a baby. She puts her hands on her belly button and tries to spread it apart to look inside. She takes out a mirror and holds it between her legs. But instead of the sweet, wrinkled old head of a teeny weeny baby, smiling and winking back at her, she only sees a little blister, just a little one, and then another, and another, and another. Baby goes to the real doctor. Where's her baby? she demands. The thing that will love her and kiss her and stay with her forever, and listen to her for the rest of her life?

The nice doctor gives Baby a teeny weeny little book that tells her all about her ugly, old disease. When she goes home, she finds Tim in the kitchen, kneeling on the floor like he's going to say a prayer. But Timmy doesn't believe in God. He's sweeping dead bug bodies into a dustpan.

She tells Tim she has just a teeny weeny case of some kind of VD. The nice doctor says it can't be cured. The nice doctor says she will have it, off and on, for the rest of her life. It's a virus. It's got a cute little nickname, "The silent partner." The silent partner stays inside you for years and years, and only once in a while does it decide to come on out and say something. It's a disease just like Tim. It's very quiet. Nobody knows it's there until it erupts, blistering and festering like a sour case of love. Baby bursts into tears. She can't go on with this story.

Tim stares down at the dustpan. Vaguely, he enjoys the evidence of his destruction. Insects deserve to die. And just that day, he found something new when he was sweeping under the sink, a pregnant mama cockroach, flattened and dessicated, her shell all crusty and her stomach split open, the skinny brown sliver of an egg poking out. Tim holds the mama cockroach in his hand now. He holds it over his left breast, like a military badge of courage. He smiles a little, for Baby, because, after all, this somewhat sloppily ends off her story. It's the last piece of the jigsaw, petrified, just like Tim, and just as out of place.

Resurrection

She was playing *Scarbo* that summer I fell in love with her. Every afternoon I walked past her brownstone and glanced up at her windows, where her Siamese cat, Philip, sat placidly behind the billowing lace panel curtains. Soft strains of music floated from her house. The sound of her piano was overridden by the rush of traffic, and since I couldn't stand still on the sidewalk to listen, I caught only a series of quick chords as I strolled up the avenue, and a long, drawn-out trill on the way back.

The Friday I had my piano lesson I almost bumped into her as she came out of the florist shop, a spray of black-eyed Susans in her hand. I hid behind a display of palm trees and then followed at a distance, keeping close enough behind so I was never out of earshot of her low-slung pumps tapping the sidewalk, brisk as a metronome's tick. Her stocking seams climbed the back of her calves off-center, and the hem of her navy dress swished. When she reached her house, I hung back at the corner, watching her transfer the bouquet of flowers from one hand to the other. She pulled an envelope out of her mailbox. Maybe it was a letter from her "absent husband," as my mother referred to the man Madame Novitski once had been, and perhaps still was, married to. On the other hand, the envelope could have been just a bill.

The great wooden door of the brownstone closed behind her. My heart thumped as I continued down the street to her house.

"Following someone, little brother?" a voice mocked.

I turned. My brother Lorenz had sneaked up behind me. "I have a lesson," I said, holding out my music to prove it.

"Still, I've seen you walk this way before, and not always on Fridays. I'm beginning to think someone might have a crush on Madame Poleski."

"*Novitski*. And I don't have a crush on her."

"Oh, then you must *esteem* her, from the front and the behind. Sideways, too, I guess she's caught your respect."

I shoved Lorenz on the shoulder. But he was seventeen and bound for pre-med school, hoping to become a psychiatrist. Whereas a year ago he would have knocked me to the pavement and pummeled my face, now he felt it beneath him to even shove me back.

"Your aggressive reaction only confirms your deeply-rooted insecurities," he informed me.

"So that explains why you beat me up when I was small," I said. "Because you felt overwhelmed by my brilliance."

Lorenz, at a loss for words, told me to get laid.

I was fifteen years old. It was my most fervent wish, and Lorenz didn't have to aspire to psychiatry to find it out. We shared a room at home, and maybe he had swung the door open a moment too early when he returned home at night from one of his rendezvous, and caught the last of one of my half-moans, half-prayers to God to send me a woman who would put me out of my misery. Maybe he had swung the door open and caught me at other things. Maybe, and most likely, he just wanted to rub in his experience, the way he once had knocked me to the floor and rubbed his dirty underwear in my face. What else were older brothers good for?

Lorenz looked up at Madame Novitski's windows, where Philip was delicately licking his front paw. He sighed. "See you at home, little brother," he said. "Give Madame Brigitte Bardotski a kiss for me." He continued down the street.

The air was unseasonably hot for early June. Several cars passed before I got up the courage to stop staring at the cracks in the sidewalk and walk up the brownstone steps. Philip meowed and jumped from the windowsill when I rang the doorbell. A full minute passed before Madame opened the door a crack and peeked out, the black-eyed Susans in her hands. When she saw it was me, she opened the door to reveal Philip standing guard in the hall, his back arched and his blue eyes glaring.

"You're early," she said.

"I am?"

She lifted the cuff of her sleeve and glanced at her gold watch. "It's three o'clock. Don't we meet at three thirty?" She looked at me closely. "Oh well, it doesn't matter. Here." She held out the flowers and commanded me in the same tone of voice she told me to play *faster, slower, with more feeling,* "Smell."

I bent my nose towards the flowers and breathed in their warm fragrance. She waved me in. "Now Feel-eep, stop that hissing," she told the cat.

"I don't think he likes me," I said.

"Nonsense." She handed me the flowers and scooped up the cat in her arms. "Philip likes you, but in general, he isn't fond of company. I don't know why. Why, Philip?" She waggled one of his paws and brushed the back of her hand along his dark whiskers. "Tell me why!" He squirmed and she dropped him to the floor. "He's so secretive! I named him after my teacher, the great Isidor Philipp, because cats, like teachers, are full of mysteries." She smiled. "Who knows? Someday you may name a cat after me."

"Maybe," I said and handed her back the flowers.

"I have some coffee brewing," she said. "You'll come in and have a cup."

I nodded and followed her into the parlor. I sat down on the red plush cushions of the sofa while she went into the dining room and opened the china closet. She pulled out a jade-colored vase. "I'll draw some water for the flowers and have coffee ready in a moment. Unless you'd rather have tea?"

"No, I love coffee. Coffee's my favorite drink."

"Do you take cream and sugar?"

"I take it straight."

I thought she smiled, but before I could be sure of it she turned her back and crossed the dining room into the kitchen, her heels tapping the hardwood floor. The door swung behind her. Philip positioned himself in front of the fireplace and fixed his glassy blue eyes on me. It was as if he knew I had never tasted coffee before in my life. I glared back at him. I hoped I wouldn't gag on it.

The parlor was cool and dark. The furniture was upholstered in deep maroons and browns. The shades were drawn except for the ones in the windows facing the street. The silence of the room, the soft light and high ceilings, reminded me of a church. It struck me that Madame and I met weekly in places that were full of mystery. For besides our weekly lesson, we met at Sunday mass, where, seated in the front pew, Madame was nothing more to me than the rim of a white hat, trimmed with the halo of a crisp navy-blue ribbon.

I hated church. I wasn't sure I believed, and as I ignored the proceedings of the mass to stare at the stained-glass windows or to tap my fingers in rhythm on my knees, I felt my mother glaring at me from behind her black chapel veil. She didn't know how my faith in God was strengthened not by the hocus-pocus the priest performed on the Eucharist, but by Madame's turning and half smiling to acknowledge me. She didn't know how much I hated to be prodded into the aisle like an obedient cow to receive Communion, embarrassed to pass Madame, who remained seated. If she had any idea how much I longed to stay behind and reject the ungrateful God who refused to embrace Madame, my mother would have given up all hope for me.

Although she hid her feelings remarkably well, my mother had taken an instant dislike to Madame the first time she brought me to this brownstone when I was thirteen. The air outside was chilly, but the parlor was warm, with a fire blazing behind the screen. Madame met us at the door. She introduced us to her indifferent cat as if he were a person. Trying to mask her distaste for animals, my mother nodded at Philip and declared him a handsome creature. My mother frowned when Madame divested me of my coat. She helped me not as if I were too young to do it myself, but the way a man would help a woman.

"You have a large family," my mother said, stepping up to the mantel to examine Madame's portraits.

"Those are composers," I said, embarrassed that my mother hadn't recognized Schubert's plump face and Beethoven's scowl.

"I don't have family anymore," Madame said. "Besides, my musical family was always more of a comfort to me than my real one."

My mother placed the sacredness of her family above all. Madame's statement struck her as blasphemy. She came to resent Madame's ideas and blamed them on her overly fancy European education. She grudged Madame's lack of real family photographs (did she have no past? or was she ashamed of it?), her title (Madame, my eye! and who was she married to, anyway?), and her fancy red plush sofa with the carved, claw-foot legs. "That sofa looks like it belongs in a bordello," she said.

"It does not," I said.

"And the smell of perfume on that woman," my mother insisted, "is like the atom bomb. It's enough to knock you over."

My mother grudged Madame her hold on me. My father, more practical, resented Madame's cost of two dear dollars an hour. "Is she giving piano lessons or running a cathouse?" he asked, as he reluctantly pulled the bills out of his wallet.

Lorenz sniggered. "If it's a cathouse, the going price for the Madame is still pretty cheap."

The more Madame rose in my estimation, the less she won of my family's esteem. I watched her emerge from behind the door. She set the vase of black-eyed Susans on the dining room table. She went back into the kitchen and came out balancing two hot steaming cups on thin saucers. As she crossed the room, I wondered how anyone could possibly find something improper about her. Her navy dress was the right length, an inch below the knee, and long-sleeved in spite of the season. The brightest thing she wore was a white collar and tiny diamond earrings that glinted slyly through her long black hair, which fell loose down her shoulders. Even if she did have the figure of Brigitte Bardot, she still dressed no differently than my mother.

"Here you go," Madame said. I took the cup and saucer she held out and balanced it on my thigh. She sat down beside me, leaving an inch of space between us on the cushion. I breathed in and the soft, powdery smell my mother so ungraciously compared to the atom bomb mingled with the aroma of the coffee. Madame's fragrance was like that of an unknown flower. I knew when I lay my head down on the pillow that night I would recall it and be filled with a sense of emptiness and unbearable longing.

I brought my cup to my mouth and took a hasty sip. The coffee scalded my tongue.

"Careful," she warned. "It's still hot."

I swallowed, and pressed my tongue against the back of my teeth. "Mmm," I said, imitating my father's words in the morning. "Strong. Just the way I like it."

She placed her cup and saucer on the dark wooden table in front of us. Philip trotted over to the sofa. When he jumped into her lap, the hem of her navy dress hiked to her knee, revealing the lace trim of her slip. The slip was aqua blue. I focused my eyes on the cat to avoid looking at it.

Madame scratched the back of Philip's head. "My goodness, Philip!" she said. "How devoted you are!"

Philip purred. I reached out my hand to touch him and he hissed.

"And so hostile to guests!" she said. "That's very impolite of you, Philip. Apologize. Apologize."

Philip looked bored.

"I guess he doesn't like me," I said.

Madame sighed and reached over her cat to retrieve her coffee cup. "How could anyone not like you? Here, Philip, let Karl touch you. Go ahead, touch him. He won't bite."

I reached out my hand and stroked his soft, golden brown fur gingerly, as if it might break. I scratched Philip's head until the silence in the parlor became unbearable, and then I took my hand away.

"Don't you like cats?" Madame asked.

"My mother doesn't like them," I said, "so we've never had one."

"Until I got Philip, I never liked cats either."

"Did you find him?"

"Oh no! This is a very expensive breed, I'm told. Stanley brought him home one day."

Stanley? I resisted the urge to say his name aloud and to ask if he was the absent husband.

Philip blinked. As Madame stroked his head with her free hand, he purred. "Philip keeps me company," Madame said. "I can't imagine what life would be like without him. You're lucky to have such a large family."

"There's just me and my parents," I said.

"And your brother," she said. "I've seen your brother in church. What is his name?"

"Lorenz," I told her, reluctantly.

"Lorenz," Madame repeated. "You're lucky to have Lorenz. Why are you making such a face?"

I felt my cheeks flush red. "Lorenz and I fight a lot."

"That's only natural," Madame said. "He's probably as bright as you, and as talented."

"He's tone deaf."

"Oh really? That's very interesting. Still, I'm sure he's good at other things besides music. I spoke with your mother after mass last Sunday. She said he was going to medical school."

"He almost didn't get in to Columbia. He got a *B* in chemistry."

"I'm sure he'll do just fine."

"I'm sure he will, too," I said. I finished my coffee, which had grown cold, and set the cup and saucer down on the table. Madame did the same.

"And you," Madame said, looking me so straight in the eye I had to look down. I caught a glimpse of her slip and then returned her gaze as best as I could. "You have much to look forward to. With plenty of work, you can count on having a successful career. But you must practice, and always practice harder and harder, every day."

I nodded, watching her tiny diamond earrings glisten behind her dark hair. Women don't just buy diamond earrings for themselves, I thought. They, too, must have been a present from Stanley.

"Shall we begin?" Madame asked. I stood up. Madame lowered Philip to the floor gently.

The lace curtains billowed back into the room and grazed the lid of the piano, which was propped open halfway. I sat down at the piano and adjusted the bench. For a moment the black and white keys swam in front of my eyes. I hated imperfection. I was always afraid to begin. I took a breath before I launched into a five-finger exercise. After half a minute she stopped me.

"No, no!" She shook her head. "Better, but still all wrong. Off the bench!"

I rose and stood behind her as she took my place at the piano. Without looking at me, she reached behind and squeezed my hand encouragingly, which was her habitual way of telling me I had my faults but wasn't a complete failure. I hung my head as she played through the exercise slowly, stopping at points and commanding me to observe where the fingers were in relation to one another, the arch of the knuckles, the proper amount of tension in the wrists. She parodied me, holding her wrists high and her fingers straight as a board. Then she relaxed her hands and the notes flowed smoothly, defying my knowledge that each key had to be struck individually. I ached inside. I would never get it right. I would never get into music school. I would never get anything I wanted.

"Now you try," she said, rising. "Imitate me."

Imitate Madame? It was an impossible task, but pleasurably so, because when she despaired of me she stood behind me and clasped my wrists, leaning her weight onto my back. "I'm guiding you," she said, patiently. "Just as I would guide a baby."

Her hair on my shoulders, her arms around me, her breasts pressed against me. How I loved her! And certainly, to embrace me that way, she had to return my love. Yes, she loved me back.

After an hour and a half of advice and corrections, she sat to my left on the bench, our thighs pressed together and our elbows rubbing. "A good lesson," she said. "Still all wrong, but much, much better."

My face flushed. I reached up to the rack and gathered my music together. She lifted the sleeve of her dress and glanced at her watch. "Will you be late getting home?" she asked.

"What time is it?"

"Four fifty-five."

"Oh no," I lied, thinking of my mother, who was probably at that moment putting dinner on the table. "We never eat until six."

"I never stop to think about other people's dinner hours. I don't really keep one myself."

"You don't eat dinner?"

"It's an informal affair. I only have myself to think of."

"You mean you just eat a peanut butter sandwich or something?"

She laughed. "You sound shocked. I've heard people say that nothing is more important to boys than what they eat for dinner." I started to protest, but she interrupted me. "Well, in any case, I can cook. Someday you'll stay for dinner, just so I can prove it. I'll invite your whole family."

"My parents never eat out," I said.

"Then just you and your brother."

"Lorenz is a picky eater. He probably wouldn't like what you cooked."

"Well, then if your mother doesn't mind, I'll steal just you for dinner."

"Okay."

The curtains, drawn back by the suction of the wind, blew in towards the screen. From the street came sounds of traffic, sudden stops, doors slamming, cars honking. I didn't move. Madame said, "I'd like to start playing some duets with you. I'd like to do some Ravel. I'm playing a piece by him now," she said, smoothing down her skirt. "A section of *Gaspard de la nuit*."

"Oh," I said, as if she weren't telling me something I already knew.

"The section is called *Scarbo*. It's very difficult. Do you know the story that inspired it? It's about an ugly dwarf who whirls madly in the air like a top, trying to reach complete happiness, but who never succeeds because the gods have cast a spell on him. Every time he comes close, he tumbles in a heap on the ground and never reaches his object."

"Is it a fairy tale?" I asked, wishing I knew it.

"A French one. But it sounds more like a tale for adults than children, doesn't it? Although I remember when I was a child, every disappointment was as crushing as death." She laughed. "Oh well. The older you get, the easier it is to resurrect yourself. Now let's look at that duet." She went over to the shelf and retrieved a tattered folio. She sat down beside me again and opened the yellow, crumpled music. The name of the piece was the *Mother Goose Suite*, and the music was heavily marked up with handwriting other than Madame's. "We'll just read through this once," she said. "At half tempo."

We began. The piece opened with a melody like a lullaby, slow and repetitious. I phrased it badly, but we came out together in the end. We continued, with *Tom Thumb* and *The Ugly Empress of the Pagodas*, *Beauty and the Beast*, and then we started on *The Enchanted Garden*. It was a quiet piece that crescendoed slowly and ponderously, the chords building up, from *piano* to *mezzo forte* to *forte*. The final crescendo was a series of glissandos assigned to my hand. It hurt to drag my thumb two octaves down the keyboard and my third finger back up. I finished off the beat after Madame already had struck what was supposed to be the final, decisive chord. I looked up at her in apology. She gazed down at the piano. "Your finger is bleeding," she said.

I looked down. The keyboard was streaked with a swipe of red. From the force of my upward glissando, the cuticle on my third finger had torn and was beaded with blood. Madame quickly took my hand in her hand and held the blood back by pressing down on my finger with the flat of her thumb.

"Does it hurt?" she asked.

"No," I said. But I felt light-headed, as if I stood on the verge of something. I looked up at her. *Now*, I thought. *Now, if you had any guts, you'd kiss her. Just kiss her.*

She smiled, and her eyes grew watery. "You're such a sweet boy," she said. "Your mother is so lucky."

She let go of my finger. Blood spotted the inside of her thumb. She reached up to the rack and folded up the *Mother Goose Suite*. "I'll see you next week," she said brusquely. She seemed embarrassed. "Or maybe this Sunday, at mass."

I averted my eyes and took my music from the rack. I rose from the bench. "Maybe," I said.

"Good-bye."

Usually she saw me to the hallway and we talked for a few minutes before my sense of courtesy got the best of me and I reluctantly reached for the doorknob. That Friday as I pulled the great wooden door of the brownstone behind me, it thudded. I stood at the top of the steps, squinting in the brightness, glad of the fresh air, no matter how warm. Car after car passed. Then I ran down the steps and joined the other people on the sidewalk. I began walking home.

Just before I reached the house, I stuck my hand into my pocket and discovered, with distaste, the two smooth, wilted dollars I was supposed to have paid Madame. I wondered how much a whore cost, and where in the world you could find one.

At home the house smelled of Friday night fish and herbed mashed potatoes. The table already was cleared, and my brother and father nowhere to be seen. I found my mother pounding dough in the kitchen, the short sleeves of her cotton dress rolled to her shoulders, the skin on her upper arms shaking as she folded the dough in half over and over, pressing it down firmly with the palm of her hand. Flour clung to her apron, powdered her face, and clung to her hair.

"Where have you been?" she demanded crossly. "I kept your dinner in the oven more than half an hour."

I opened the oven and looked into its dark mouth. It was empty.

"Too late," she said. "Lorenz ate it."

"Lorenz!"

"Why are you so surprised?"

"It was my dinner."

"Maybe next time you're off cavorting at the dinner hour you'll remember your brother has a healthy appetite."

"I wasn't cavorting," I said. "I had a lesson."

"A three-hour piano lesson?" my mother said. "Madame must have been feeling generous."

I didn't answer. I opened the icebox and stared inside. My mother clucked her tongue when I pulled out some kielbasa.

"You can't have that," she said.

"Why not?"

"Meat on Friday?"

I put the kielbasa back in the icebox.

"You'd all be on the road to hell if I weren't here to watch over you," she said, wiping the sweat off her forehead with the back of her dough-encrusted hand. I sat down at the table.

"If you're not too lazy to use the can opener," she said, "there's a tin of tuna fish in the cabinet."

"I'm not hungry."

She hummed a little tune to herself, then said, "Funny how men are never hungry unless women are willing to wait on them."

"I'm just not hungry," I said.

"Suit yourself."

Nothing made her more angry than our being late to dinner. And although she complained about how little we appreciated her cooking, nothing made her more pleased than to see Lorenz and me eat. "Spoiled," she often said, as we shoveled it down. "But healthy. Just the way I want my boys to be."

She slapped the dough over and over again onto the table. After a while she looked up. "What's the matter?" she asked.

"Nothing."

"Do you feel sick?"

I shook my head.

"So why don't you eat something?"

"Because it's Friday, Mother," Lorenz's voice rang out behind me. I turned and saw him smirking in the doorway. "And on Fridays Karl experiences the normal reaction of any depraved Catholic boy: denied meat, he craves only meat, and loses desire for fish."

My mother stared at Lorenz. "Ever since you've gotten the brilliant idea to become a psychiatrist, you've gone crazy."

"Karl understands what I mean."

"I do not," I said.

"Talk sense," my mother told Lorenz, "or I'm warning you, I'll wash your mouth out with soap."

Lorenz laughed. The doorbell rang and he left the kitchen to meet his date, one of an endless string of nameless, faceless girls that he regularly entertained on the front porch swing in warm weather, and in the winter, in the back seat of borrowed cars. This one's voice was high-pitched and broken with intermittent giggles. Within thirty seconds of being greeted by Lorenz, she was crying, "Stop it, Renzie!"

"Renzie?" my mother echoed, looking up from her dough. She frowned, then resumed pounding. "That Lorenz," she said. "He'll get some girl in trouble, and then what?"

"At least he'll have fun doing it," I said.

She glared at me. Then she reached across the table and squinched my cheek with one of her floured hands. "You're worse than your brother. Not worth the trouble of raising you Catholic."

She released her grip on me. I tried to wipe the flour off my face, but it clung to my skin like a beard. "Why aren't you shaving?" my mother demanded.

I shrugged to stall time before admitting, "Lorenz said I'd look better if I grew a mustache."

She sighed. "Some people are born with good looks," she said. "Other people have to live with the looks they're born with."

"Like me."

"Your looks are not so bad." She crossed the kitchen and retrieved her bread molds from the hooks on the wall. She began to grease the molds with butter. I pressed my thumb onto the layer of flour on the table and left a fingerprint.

"The whole world stinks," I said.

"So when did you find that out?" she asked. "Just yesterday?"

"I guess I've known it all along."

"So know it and then make up your mind to forget about it."

"I can't. You shouldn't. Why should people forget about it?"

She knocked flour around the sides of the molds. "Then get a megaphone and start announcing it on the streets. See how long it takes before they lock you up." She cut the dough into separate portions and whacked each into their individual molds. "Don't look so grim," she said. "You'll be happy someday."

I slouched in my chair and stuck my hands into my pockets. I fingered the dollar bills and my face flushed. "When?" I asked.

"You'll be married. Have your own house. Family."

"I'll never get married."

"Be a priest, then, and do God some good."

"I don't want to be a priest," I said.

"When you're young, you don't know what you want."

"I know what I want."

"Well, what is it then?" my mother asked, clattering the pans full of dough down on the counter.

"I want to be anything other than what I am."

She stared out the window into the backyard. I was sure she would begin lecturing me about being grateful to God for God's gifts. Instead, she looked down at her dirty apron and her flour-encrusted fingers. "That I can understand," she said.

I slouched down further in my chair. How could she possibly understand? Unless she wanted to be something other than what she was. But my mother couldn't possibly be dissatisfied with who she was, because if she wasn't who she was, she never would have given birth to me. I wouldn't be there. I wouldn't exist. My head ached with the thought. I was confused. Here was Madame saying she wanted me as her son, and my own mother practically saying she never wanted me. When your own mother didn't want to cook you dinner or bake you bread, the whole world really did stink. But somehow you had to find a way to live with it.

I pushed back my chair. I left the kitchen and wandered out into the garden. I crossed the lawn towards the plum tree and sat down in a wrought-iron chair. The garden was a hotbed of fragrances, of hyacinth, snapdragons, peonies, gardenias. Twilight cast long shadows across the lawn and the scent of flowers grew stronger as the air grew more still. From the kitchen came the sounds of pans rattling and clanking as my mother washed up. My father's voice wafted across the lawn as he called from upstairs for my mother.

"Monica. Monica."

"I'll be up in a minute."

I lay my head back in the chair and stared at the reddening sky. I longed to grow up. But if I couldn't grow up and feel good about myself, I would settle for having someone who accepted and wanted me. Madame? She was the closest and farthest woman from my mind. She knew too much! She saw me as I was, a skinny, eager boy, who would always remain eager, probably, until he found some plain-looking, devoted young wife. What would she want with me? If I kissed her, she would evaluate it the way she evaluated the execution of a C major scale: *Better, better, but still all wrong.* I shuddered with embarrassment, and hoped I hadn't given myself away. I would have to be content with what I could get, and some girl that would be. A girl more devoted to her piano or her violin than to her husband, a girl who had to keep her fingernails clipped to the quick in order to properly respond to her instrument's touch, a girl to whom earrings, bracelets, and rings were strictly forbidden. She would know how to make love to her instrument better than to any man. And yet she would be a girl, my girl, and she would love me.

Such luck seemed far off. I could hardly sit in my chair thinking of the lonely, unfortunate time to come. I got up. If I walked by Madame's brownstone, she would be playing *Scarbo*, the same as always. Philip would be sitting in the window. Maybe she would welcome me back inside. Maybe. I crossed the lawn and stopped by one of the flower beds by the house. A perfectly shaped yellow rose bloomed on one of the bushes. I bent over its petals and breathed in its beautiful fragrance. Carefully avoiding the thorns, I bent the stem and snapped the flower off.

Inside the house, my parents were nowhere to be seen. The dining room, the parlor, the kitchen stood empty. I walked into the kitchen and took a glass from the cabinet. I filled it with water and stuck the rose inside. It toppled to one side of the glass and looked bare and forlorn. I opened the other cabinets, looking for a vase.

From the front porch I heard Lorenz's girlfriend giggle, and then Lorenz's low voice, cajoling her along. I decided I hated my brother. I couldn't think of where my mother might keep a vase. The silence in the house was eerie. I wanted to be with Madame. Upstairs, I heard my parents' bed creak. It only creaked once, but it reminded me of where I came from and made me wonder where I was going.

I left the flower resting in the water glass. It seemed as if everyone knew how to seize what they wanted, except for me. The air was moist with the smell of yeast. I looked down into the metal molds which held the dough for the bread. The dough was the sickly, pasty color of flesh. I felt the coffee Madame had served me coursing through my body as I grabbed one of the molds, made a fist, and sank it deep in the dough. "Stop rising!" I commanded it. "Just stop rising!"

Second Coming

Thursday I took the train to Jersey to break the news about Claire to my brother. The train was packed, and a young man—Puerto Rican or Cuban, I couldn't tell which—stood up to offer his seat. I looked around for a pregnant woman. But there was no mistaking he stood up for me. He gestured to the bench with the same sort of flourish he might have used to wave a cape in a bull ring. I looked at my reflection in the window—sagging jowls, hangdog eyes. This was no bull staring back at me, but an old man, an aged piece of beef.

The train took off with a jolt. I sat down. *"Gracias,"* I mumbled.

"No problem, Daddy-O," he said.

The train rattled on the tracks like a loose windowpane in a windstorm. The floor, littered with chewing gum wrappers and the chalky material stuffed in cigarette filters, felt gritty beneath my feet. Across the aisle a woman hid behind a gossip sheet emblazoned with apocalyptic headlines: TWO-HEADED BABY ALIVE AND WELL, BUT SUFFERING FROM IDENTITY CRISIS! I stared at the toreador's black hooflike shoes, the kind that were in style thirty years ago, all the way to Jersey.

In spite of the sweltering heat, I would rather have stayed in the city that day. My studio was air-conditioned, no students were coming by, and I could have spent the afternoon tackling the fugue of the *Wanderer Fantasy*. In an afternoon behind the keyboard I could have sorted out my feelings as I sorted out the chords. I could have created, out of chaos, harmony. But I had to call on my brother in Ho-Ho-Kus sooner or later.

My brother Lorenz is a urologist. Last year on his twenty-fifth anniversary as a physician the hospital where he performs his surgery confiscated a kidney stone, the size of a piece of coal, that Lorenz had extracted from a well-known professional football player years before. They silver-plated it and mounted it on a block of wood like a trophy. *King of Kidneys,* the inscription read. Lorenz was deeply touched. "Nothing makes me feel more useful than relieving a man of his stones," he once confided to me, over his third beer. "They come to me in agony, Karl—their gut burning and their prick in flames! A few blasts with the laser beam, and I've extinguished the fires of hell. It makes me feel like a priest. It makes me feel holy. I was born for urology."

My personal opinion was that he was born to be full of himself. But I didn't say anything. If Lorenz wanted to think of himself as King of Kidneys, fine—I certainly wasn't going to arm-wrestle him for the title. His success I didn't grudge. He worked hard and deserved it. But I envied his comfortable life-style, and the fact that he supported a family, a dog, and two cats besides, whereas I could barely support myself. Papa had been right. "Put your hands to practical use," I heard him say, reminding me even beyond the grave that if only I had been grabbing men by the nuts all these years instead of trying to grab their attention by playing the piano, I could have had a house in Jersey, too.

"Doctors practice to make money," Papa said, "but musicians practice why? Just to keep on practicing? Makes no sense."

My mother could be counted upon to come to my defense. "Leave him alone," she said. "He's got an urge, let him follow it."

"Should he follow every urge he's got?" Papa asked. "He's got an urge to be a murderer—fine, let him kill everybody! He's got an urge to steal—then steal! He's got an urge to go with the girls—fine, let him have every Sally and Susie, without any thought of the future and the responsibilities!"

That had silenced my mother. Girls were Lorenz's vice and she was convinced girls would be Lorenz's downfall. One son who was a skirt-chaser was enough. She wanted me to practice piano not because it was an honorable or profitable thing to do, but because she thought it would keep me out of trouble. It was Lorenz's biology books, she believed, that gave her boys *ideas*. If only she could throw those books on the fire, our ideas, and not our precariously Catholic immortal souls, would eventually go up in flames.

She could have rested easy. In those days it was all ideas for me, all fantasy, and no action other than the solitary relief I found in the bedroom after everyone else in the house was either out or asleep. In those days Lorenz used to return home late from a rendezvous, sneak up the stairs, and swing open the bedroom door in hopes of catching me in the humiliating act. "Strumming on the old banjo?" he pleasantly inquired as I feigned sleep. That infuriated me enough to send me out of the sheets and into his arms, where we punched and pummeled each other until Papa came in to break it up.

Fistfights were our idea of a brotherly embrace. Looking back on it all, it seems a wonder we never injured each other's hands, the hands that would become the respective tools of our trade. While I clawed out a meager living, Lorenz had grasped a plush practice in downtown Ho-Ho-Kus, a waiting room full of leather furniture, and a nurse so devoted to his Christmas bonuses that she had been with him for twenty years. Twenty years, and still Nurse Richards never recognized me.

She happened to be behind the reception desk when I came in. "You're early, Mr. Teitelman," she said. "What's the trouble? Prostate flaring up again?"

It still smarted, after all these years, to realize that people couldn't believe I was related to my handsome brother. "But you look so dif-

ferent!" we used to hear all the time. Lorenz had won the beauty
contest with his clean, chiseled looks. My looks have—well, plenty
of *character*.

"I'm here to see my brother," I told her. She bit her lip, apologized,
and told me to have a seat inside his office. "He's straightening a rod,"
she said. I didn't bother to ask what she meant. Urology gives me the
heebie-jeebies. Doctors make me squeamish, and Lorenz, in his white
coat, gives me the creeps. My worst fear is of being rushed to the hospital and finding myself at his mercy. In a horrible nightmare I once
had, Lorenz leaned over my hospital gurney. "Pain in the groin?" he
asked in his cheerful voice. "I'm afraid we'll have to amputate."

What a dream. I woke up to find I had kicked the blankets off
the bed. I stayed awake until the gray light of morning and the rattle
of taxicabs speeding down the street below lulled me back into an
uneasy sleep.

I followed Nurse Richards down the carpeted hall and let myself
into Lorenz's office, a shrine that celebrated the pains and pleasures
of masculinity. On his desk, next to the silver-plated kidney stone,
he kept a stone spiked like a child's jack. "Paperweight," he showed
it off, with satisfaction. The spikes of the stone, so fragilely formed,
were wrapped in the sandy, slatelike colors of a nursery: creams, pale
blues, and pinks. It was hard to believe such a pretty little thing had
once wreaked so much havoc in a man's system. The stones represented the agonies. Behind his desk, in a glass case, he kept his
homage to the ecstacies: an exhibit of the various penile prostheses,
miracle workers for the impotent man, godsends to the needy. "I once
implanted one of these in an eighty-three-year-old man," Lorenz told
me, "and imagine—he wanted it to be outpatient surgery. Whoopee!"

One afternoon around last Christmas, while my stomach grumbled
and I impatiently waited for Lorenz to take me home to dinner, he
spent a quarter of an hour demonstrating how the prostheses worked.
He was like a child showing off his new toys. "And then you pump this

little gizmo like this . . . and inflate this little gitchee like that . . . and
the male member is miraculously transformed from a limp noodle into
an exploding rocket, a veritable Excalibur, hard as steel! These are
the most wonderful gadgets ever invented. Forget Alexander Graham
Bell. Forget the light bulb."

"That was Edison."

He glared at me. "Never mind the flushing toilet. This invention
has saved many a man's pride. If you know anyone who's having
problems—"

"I don't."

"Who's accusing you?" he said.

"I was—I mean, you are—always bugging me about women."

He began to put his gadgets away. "I'm just curious. I mean, it's
been a while. Why not get remarried?"

"If I meet a woman, I'll marry a woman. I can't spend half my life
wandering around looking for one."

"Bets and I are worried about you," he said. "We'd like to see you
settle down. Have a real home. A wife."

"Those things don't just fall out of the sky. You have to be lucky."

Lorenz gave a final loving pat to one of the prostheses before he
closed the glass case. "You should stop dating those fly-by-nights.
Can't you find someone solid?"

"It's a fly-by-night world," I said, more to make him question his
enviable long marriage to Bets than to voice any firm belief of my
own. "No one's into commitment."

That hit him where it hurt. "You're too old to be chasing women,"
he said. "Besides, I just don't understand why they always fall for
your sad-eyed face."

"I'm sensitive. They like the artist type."

"Art doesn't put dinner on the table."

"You sound like Papa," I said. "And you're beginning to look like
him, too."

47

Lorenz clutched his well-padded stomach. "Not so! Papa looked like he was pregnant!" We spent the next five minutes climbing on and off the office scale, comparing his 185 pounds to my 147, his tall frame to my compact one. We called in Nurse Richards to measure our waists with a tape. She refused, pronouncing us a couple of overgrown babies.

That was last Christmas. Now I took a seat in front of Lorenz's desk. To the left hung a poster illustrating the function of the prostate gland, and to the right, a poster of the entire male reproductive system. Lorenz probably dreamed of urethras and bladders and testicles the way I dreamed of music. His subconscious must be swimming with spermatozoa, his dreams haunted by failed erections, his nightmares ruled by visions of faulty chromosomes, chromosomes that—alas!—had produced only daughters. It bothered Lorenz that he never had a son. "I know it's illogical," he once told me, "but I resent Bets for it." Maybe that was why he hung the poster in such a prominent place, to remind himself that he, and only he, was responsible for releasing the X or Y chromosomes into the furtiveness of the night to make their secret journey.

Now those chromosomes were my goddaughters and nieces, Lorenz's once so darling and now so maladjusted teenage girls. Dina and Donna were always on the run, to and from ballet lessons, skating lessons, piano lessons—none of which seemed to do them any good. They remained clumsy and graceless as ever, and the stilted recitals of *Für Elise* and *Polonaise Militaire* they occasionally blundered through for my benefit were nothing short of torture.

They were such healthy, pretty girls, made ugly by the disdain on their faces and the alarming amount of cosmetics they felt obliged to wear. I bored them as much as they amused me. "Oh *hi*, Uncle Karl," they finally acknowledged me after galloping into the house, fighting about some boy or other who Donna absolutely *loved* but who Dina knew was absolutely *off limits*. I brought little glamour into their lives, even though I hailed from the city their mother rarely allowed them to visit.

"Do you wear a tuxedo to all the concerts at Carnegie Hall?" they asked.

"That's for the rich benefactors," I said. "I'm just a lover of music."

"Guess our dad would wear a tuxedo."

"Girls, I guess your dad would fall asleep."

"That's true. He always says he wishes you would play something jumpy and jazzy instead of dull old Beethoven."

I was expected to bring them fashion reports back from the city; instead, I brought them volumes of Jane Austen and Charlotte Bronte for birthdays and Christmas, for which I received halfhearted written acknowledgments in the mail. "Dear Uncle Karl, Thank you for the books. We have so much homework we're not sure when we'll have time to read them. They'll look nice up on the shelf with all the other ones you've given us. Can't wait to see you again." Finally I gave up and let Bets, Lorenz's wife, do the shopping for me. She obviously doubled the money I gave her to buy the girls gifts, because they always came wrapped in boxes from Saks and Lord & Taylor's. Suddenly I was receiving warm hugs and sloppy kisses for the expensive wool skirts and 18-karat gold jewelry that came as much as a surprise to me as it did to them. "Thank you so much, Uncle Karl, we love you and wish you'd stop smoking so much, because Dad says if you don't do it, pretty soon you'll drop dead."

The private information those girls so often let slip caused me to cherish them. "Mom says you probably eat breakfast at a Chock-Full-O-Nuts every morning because you don't have someone to fix it for you. She says maybe you should have stayed married to Aunt Rosalie because then at least you'd have clothes that matched and pressed shirts." They were obsessed with Rosalie, and apparently, so were Lorenz and Bets. "Dad told us Aunt Rosalie was one hot potato. Mom

said she was the kind that exploded in the oven. Then Dad said Mom
never liked her anyway and Mom said that didn't matter because Dad
liked her double for the both of them. Then they acted kind of snotty
to each other for a couple of days, and when Dad came back from the
urology convention we could hardly sleep because he snored on the
couch *all night long*."

"Great kids," I often told Lorenz. "You truly deserve them."

After five minutes or so, Lorenz burst into the office, his voice
booming, the tails of his white coat streaming behind. "Karl, old
buddy!" he said as I stood up. "Got a great ha-ha for you. Why did
the delivery boy get AIDS?" He waited for me to shrug. "Because
he thought it was safe to come in the back door!" He slapped me on
the back, shook my hand too vigorously, and like the toreador on the
train, motioned for me to sit down again. He flopped into his leather
desk chair. Lorenz had a great feel for the dramatic. Everything he did
was just a little exaggerated, as if he were playing to a full house and
everyone's eyes were riveted on him.

He complained of his day, all the while aware that what had been
minor annoyances to him were the stuff theater was made of for his
patients. He knew that when they returned home from his office they
called their relatives and friends, turning every wart and lump and
scratch on their bodies into life-and-death situations. He knew they
quoted him verbatim, repeating, "My doctor said . . . my doctor
said . . ." Picking up the jack-shaped kidney stone off his desk, I let
him ramble.

"—at the hospital all morning when this half-hour job turned into
a two-hour procedure. Then Christ Almighty, the capper came right
when I was flying out the door and they delivered this hermaphrodite kid." I looked up. Lorenz winked. "It's got characteristics of
both sexes—they call it ambiguous genitalia. So they send me in to
tell the parents they have the choice whether to name the kid Dick—

pardon the pun—or Sally. A real hunky-dory of a headache, believe
you me. What's wrong, Karl? You're squirming in your seat. Hemorrhoids acting up again?"

Would he never let me live down those hemorrhoids? "No. I just
feel for the parents of that baby, that's all."

"Don't bother. We can fix it." He rocked in his desk chair. "What
a life! You really look sick. Sure you're all right? Blood pressure up?
Students giving you an ulcer? *More liquids.* Drink more liquids and
try not to take life so seriously." He stared at me. "What's the matter?
Bad news?"

I shook my head. I nodded.

His face paled and his voice lowered. "You don't have . . ." He
paused. "Oh God, all those years of smoking. Is it the Big C?"

"Don't be ridiculous," I said. "The thing is . . . it's like this . . .
Well, listen. I'm getting married," I said, and set the jack-shaped
kidney stone down on his desk with a decisive bang.

"Careful with that stone!" He swiveled forward on his chair and
rescued it. "This one is very rare, it's type—"

"Lor, did you hear me?"

"Of course." Satisfied I hadn't injured the stone, he set it back
down. "Married to what? Who?"

"To this woman I'm seeing."

"You're seeing a woman?"

"No, I'm seeing a chimpanzee."

He grinned. "That's a step down from Rosalie."

If it wasn't the hemorrhoids, it was Rosalie he couldn't stop throwing up to my face. "Claire isn't down from Rosalie. She's quality stuff.
As far from Rosalie as you can get."

"You don't want to go too far. Rosalie had her good points. Small
tits, but nice ass."

"Do you mind?"

But Lorenz was oblivious to his own crudeness. "So tell me how far is far, little brother."

Guilt overcame me whenever I thought of Rosalie and Claire in the same breath. Not that I hadn't compared them a hundred times before—mostly to reassure myself I wasn't repeating the same mistakes—but I had never done it out loud, with someone else before. It took a moment to get over my shyness.

So Claire was tall, and Rosalie, tiny. Claire—and everything about Claire—spelled softness, from her pale skin to her wavy blond hair, whereas Rosalie—and everything about Rosalie—the sharp nose, the cheekbones, the chic, angular body—spelled severity. Claire was reserved; Rosalie was outgoing. Claire kept it in and Rosalie spilled it out. Claire was modest and Rosalie—

"—was a slut and a half," Lorenz finished for me.

"How do you know?"

Lorenz smiled and folded his hands like a priest. "I have an imagination."

And so did I, an imagination that had always conjured up visions of Rosalie with other men. She flirted with everyone, even Lorenz. Lorenz had been taken with her; Bets, smelling her out in a single sniff, had despised her from the very beginning. Bets would approve of Claire, though, because Claire would never sidle up to Lorenz. Already she dreaded meeting him. "Nothing personal," Claire said, "but I just don't like doctors."

"Lorenz definitely fits the mold," I said. "Just keep your distance and we'll all be safe."

I told both her and Lorenz so many exaggerations about each other that when the two finally met they would probably feel as though they were walking on the moon for the first time. The unexpected loss of gravity. The giddiness of the rise, with none of my impressions to anchor them. Claire would pinch me on the arm afterwards and say,

"Why, he's not so bad after all. And she's charming, his wife. And the girls . . ." Her forehead would furrow. "The girls will be girls, as girls will be."

Polite of her. Claire was courteous. She dressed in a small-town way—dresses gathered at the waist, low-heeled pumps, and flesh-colored stockings. She was thrifty. She served meat loaf for dinner and pound cake for dessert. She washed the crumbs out of plastic bread bags and hung them on the wash line. She poured grease into a coffee can. If she used an egg yolk for one recipe, she found a way to use the white in another. She was such a calm, peaceful person that when she came into the city she seemed overwhelmed more by the sharp, noisy people who surrounded her than by the skyscrapers. She would never learn how to own the sidewalk. She looked provincial as an immigrant from the 1930s. But what could you expect from the church organist in Bayetteville, upstate New York?

"She doesn't sound like your type," Lorenz said.

"I'm not sure that she is."

"So what the hell are you marrying her for?"

I cleared my throat. "She's pregnant."

Lorenz really did remind me of Papa sometimes. He slapped the desk. "You're fifty years old!"

"Don't remind me."

"I told you years ago, come in for a vasectomy."

"But I've always wanted children."

"To do what, dig your grave? How old is she, anyway? Fourteen?"

"Thirty-seven."

"Good-looking?"

"She wears silk underwear."

Lorenz whistled a low note. And then, as if he were right on top of me, about to stick a tongue depressor in my mouth, or flash a light in my eye, I heard his heavy, measured breathing rising and falling like a repeated musical phrase. "Bets wears those ugly cotton things."

"I know."

"How?"

"I saw them hanging in the bathroom last time I visited."

Lorenz sighed. When he was a boy and Mama grounded him to the house for some misdeed, he always sat in the rocking chair by the fireplace and restlessly tilted out his frustrations. Now his dissatisfaction was apparent in the way he rocked back and forth in his desk chair.

"I love Bets," he said, "but I'm miserable."

"Don't do anything rash," I said. "I count on you for stability." It was true. Ever since Mama and Papa died, Lorenz and Bets had been like a father and mother to me. They were the force to which I was accountable, my Thanksgiving and Christmas and birthday dinners.

"Stability," Lorenz said. He lingering on each syllable. "Wait until you have a family, and you'll find out how stable stability can get. You'll find yourself worrying about lawn mowers and front door locks and termites in the garage. You'll wake up in the morning with your mind on the rising price of gas and electricity, and when you don't dream about the furnace and the dishwasher, you'll be dreaming about one-way trips to Bermuda and Jamaica. You'll go nuts. I swear I'm crazy. You'll love your wife but you'll want to fuck the baby-sitter. You'll love your kids but they'll make you wonder why you ever fucked your wife. And your house. It's supposed to be your castle, right? Wrong. It's your own personal home for the insane. God, I live in a nuthouse. When Bets isn't having hot flashes, the girls are on the rag. When they aren't at each other's throats, they're all ganged up on me. They want a dog, another cat, a new prom dress, and this or that shade of nail polish is *ab-so-lute-ly essential, Daddy,* if they're going to keep on living another single second. They want me to be friendlier, they want me to be more fatherly, they want me to stop talking about laser beams and circumcision, but it's fine for them to suffocate me in a sea of pantyhose and perfume and endless talk about their periods at the dinner table. I ask you, do I look like I care about things like that?"

The veins in Lorenz's neck bulged out. I smiled. "Gee, I had no idea you were so unhappy," I said.

He brooded over that for a moment. Then he swiveled, full circle, in his chair, and when he returned to his original position his calm, doctorly facade once again ruled. "Have a boy, Karl. It's the only sensible thing to do."

"You can't order up the big things on prescription, Lor."

"Too bad. We'd all be a lot happier."

"We don't know what's good for us, anyhow."

Two sharp knocks came on the door. Nurse Richards stuck in her head. "Mr. Teitelman is here with his prostate."

Poor Mr. Teitelman. I imagined him in the adjoining examination room, cradling his aching prostate in his arms like a newborn baby, waiting for Lorenz's sage words on how to nurse it.

Lorenz stood up. "Congratulate my brother, Nurse Richards—he's going to be a father."

It was so like Nurse Richards to speak to Lorenz and not to me. "I thought he was a bachelor."

"He doesn't believe in wasting time. He's on his way to Macy's to shop for both the teddy bear and the engagement ring."

Nurse Richards narrowed her eyes at me and walked out.

"Did you have to do that?" I asked.

Lorenz laughed. He opened the door of the examination room. "Wait here. After this appointment, the doctor will order his brother a drink."

The door closed. I sighed, captive to Lorenz's will and his loud voice, which rang clearly through the thin walls. "Mr. Teitelman! How's the old ball game today?"

Mr. Teitelman had a thin, reedy voice. "I used to think being a widower was the only thing I had to kvetch about, Doctor, but ever since this pain started up . . ."

"Why don't you just lie down on the table and relax. Relax. You think you got it bad? My brother's in the next room. He's fifty years old and he just knocked up the church organist. Is that *schlemiel* or what?"

"He doesn't know what trouble he's in for."

"Relax. Relax."

Mr. Teitelman was right. I had no idea, even though Lorenz had just offered up his jaded inkling. I was stepping off a plane without a parachute; I was plunging into the depths without the ability to swim. I had never been known to save myself. Only a miracle could keep me intact and afloat; only Claire could rescue me. Surely she (so capable, so thrifty) would pick me up and dust me off if I fell; surely she would hang me out to dry on the wash line, like a reusable plastic bag, if ever I were drowning. Claire was my guardian angel. She believed in fixing something the moment after it broke. The worst mistake she had ever made was . . . maybe to get caught up with me?

So maybe we were doing the wrong thing, condemning ourselves to the roar of the vacuum cleaner and the buzz of the lawn mower for the rest of our lives. Superfluous machinery? There was no way to know until you stood behind their handles for a while and felt them vibrating in your fingers, their energy coursing through your body like the current of an electric chair. Deathly. But potential headaches, possible blisters, even the risk of death itself suddenly seemed preferable to the silence of a solitary life. Stories of lecherous old bachelors competed with the roar of the vacuum cleaner in my head. The tales they had told of my Uncle Casimir after they sealed his coffin: he'd had his way with the ladies all his life, until one morning he woke up next to some old flame and realized he had just had the last woman of his life. The fire was out. Uncle Casimir groaned, rolled over, and drew his final breath. No, I could not let that happen to me.

Relax. Relax. Like Mr. Teitelman on the table, I sunk lower in my chair and succumbed to Lorenz's soothing voice. All about me prostates swelled and dilated, spermatozoa swam like salmon upstream. Upstream! Now that was machinery, machinery that uttered not a sound, machinery that functioned with frightening efficiency. Guaranteed that if you used your tool often enough, the hammer would hit the nail on the head, and out would pop a little John Henry. Oh, there were times when I marveled at its beauty, and times when I didn't want any part of its deviousness. The hell with these tubes and glands and ducts, the hell with Lorenz's posters that supposedly mapped my system. I didn't want a system. I wanted to be stuffed with cotton and old fishnet stockings, a starved-for-love rag doll baby.

And this baby, that was the cause of so much to-do. Who *was* this baby? He, too, seemed as fictitious as the system supposedly inside of me. He was still nothing more than that first strange, awkward, and indecisive embrace in Claire's dimly lit kitchen, when I made the age-old plea: *Let me stay.*

She shook her head. *I look like hell in the morning.*

That's all right. I look like a basset hound. We shouldn't let such minor considerations stand in our way.

No, he was nothing more to me yet than the silliness that overtook us on the stairs, the softness of the pillows, the lazy cigarette afterwards, the rich, heavy smell of the coffee Claire dripped in the morning. He was eggs and toast and pancakes. He was the opening bars of the *Wanderer Fantasy*, the loud heraldic chords I pounded upon Claire's piano while the bacon spit on the burner, the major chords that called for even more greatness to come. He was the act and not the result. He was the oldest story ever told, the story men and women told over and over and over again, in spite of all the trouble it caused them.

He was the miraculous second coming of a miniature me. Right now, in the orchestral hall of Claire's womb, he was pounding out a fugue, his spindly little fingers playing the imaginary keys of his bony knees. Like everyone else, he was bound to suffer an identity crisis; he was bound to wither and grow old, and perhaps be in need of one of Lorenz's miracle-working gadgets someday. But by then Lorenz and I would be out of the picture.

57

I clutched the arms of my chair. A baby. Born only so I could die. Born so that someday, over breakfast, I would look across the table and see his cherub's smile, and realize I was an old man in baggy pants, as useless and flabby as the last cold pancake Claire had flopped upon my plate. It wasn't accident that made him, wasn't the horrible loneliness I desired to dispel one night, but the need to find an understudy, someone to fill in the gap in the world sure to be left when someday death, a brilliant toreador with flashing white teeth and a crisp red cape, flourished his hands and I charged into the darkness.

And for this, I was supposed to say *gracias*? I clenched my teeth together, as if preparing to fight.

But I was a sweetheart of a guy. The grateful sort, the kind who let others do the amputating, preferring to go with the flow instead. I unclenched my teeth and released my grip on the chair. I remembered lecherous Uncle Casimir had this saying, which he repeated often, with a wink. *Life got you by the balls? Death screwing you up the ass? Enjoy, enjoy!*

Uncle Casimir, God bless your soul. I closed my eyes, and while Lorenz, in an other-worldly, quiet voice repeated *relax, relax,* I offered up a sort of thanks.

Mother Rocket

So Jude Silverman was a Yiddish Chicken Little? What did it
matter, when she had Rob Jones, the man who proposed to
keep the sky, however gray, up above? He had promised her
this years ago, in a flat in Brooklyn, when Jude poised her beat-up feet
on the inside of the window ledge, clutched the drab, mud-colored
curtains, and threatened to throw her 100-pound body splat into the
street.

"Now Jude," Rob said. "Don't do that."

"I was born to die," Jude said.

"So do it later, when I'm not looking. Come on down now, and
we'll get married."

"Well." Jude looked dubious. "Okay. All right."

The marriage license they applied for an hour later seemed to ap-
pease Jude's suicidal urge, although it whetted a desire for a hot, salty
pretzel. Only a pretzel delivered from the wrinkled hands of a vendor
in Central Park would do. Jude wound her hair into a knot and kissed
Rob, long and lovingly, on the subway into the city. "Trains really
bring out something from my cultural unconscious!" she shouted
above the roar.

"Could you speak a little louder? I don't think they heard you over
on Staten Island."

Jude pouted. "You never let me feel persecuted. You never let me
feel guilty."

An hour later she was weeping over the polar bear—big, white, and shaggy—that paced its cage, like a madman, in Central Park. "He's been here as long as I can remember," she said. "He's so hot. He's so lonely. He probably has bad breath. He probably hates himself." Jude gave the polar bear a long, significant glance of farewell that signaled her identification with him was complete. She sniffled. "You got a Kleenex? This pretzel is so lousy, it's making me cry. I'm warning you. You'd better not marry me. The littlest thing sets me off."

As if Rob, the moment he met her, hadn't figured that out. It was what initially attracted him. He'd been a UPI photographer in Southeast Asia before his weak stomach had gotten the best of him and he returned to New York to shoot not battlefields and revolutions and riots, but movie stars and models and other such innocuous subjects. He was disappointed in his lack of heroics until the day he went to the theater to photograph Jude and broke down her explosive temper as expertly as a soldier might dismantle a grenade. "Load your guns," Jude had ordered him. "And don't make me look ugly. Make me look like Pavlova, you know? Or Isadora Duncan."

"I'm a photographer, not a plastic surgeon."

"What's that supposed to mean?"

"It means, be yourself."

Jude's forehead wrinkled. "But I don't know who I am."

Rob bit his lip in exasperation. "You can be a tightrope walker or a plumber. You can be a duck or an elephant, for all I care."

"Are you trying to call me schizophrenic?"

"I'm trying to get you to pose!" Rob shouted. "Would you pose, please, so I can get out of here and eat my dinner?"

Jude backed her body up to the wall as if preparing to be executed. "Okay," she said penitently. "I'll cut the ishkabibble. Fire away."

She was a principal with the Future/Dance/Theater, a modern troupe committed to catering to the so-called politically aware. The week before, Rob had seen her perform her most famous solo role, "Hiroshima," a dance consisting of nothing more than an excruciatingly slow meltdown to the stage, so that at the end of seven minutes Jude lay in a heap on the floor, symbolizing the Japanese dead. The dance was a New York hit. It was supposed to be a social statement, but Rob thought it was so much sixties kitsch. The naiveté of it offended him. "What do dancers know about politics?" he challenged Jude at that photo session.

"All we need to know: Hitler killed the Jews. Hey, you want to take me out to dinner? Feel free to say no if you're married or engaged or gay."

In the restaurant, when she wasn't stealing drags off Rob's cigarette, stuffing her mouth with grilled steak, or washing her food down with beer, she complained. "It's horrible being a dancer," she said. "You can't smoke. You can't drink. You can't eat. You can't have tits or hips, you can't have a headache or a stomachache or a backache, you can't have a social life or a family or a boyfriend—"

"Why can't you have a boyfriend?"

"You should see the fruitcakes I meet." She stared at him. "You're too old not to be married."

"So my mother tells me."

"Are you sure you're not gay?"

Rob leaned across the candlelit table, gently covered Jude's hand with his hands, and looked her meaningfully in the eye. He hoped to sound tender and eloquent and romantic. "I love women," he said.

"Great," Jude answered. "Let's get laid. But first let me finish off these croutons." She dug into her salad with her fork. "I hate when they're drowning in dressing. I feel personally responsible. I need to rescue them, every survivor. I can't leave a single one behind."

Rob was amused by her zeal. Unlike his previous subjects in New York, Jude had passion, however misguided. It didn't strike him she was disturbed until she admitted it herself, back at his place. "I'm a kook," she warned. "A real nut. No analyst would touch me with a ten-foot pole."

"I'm not an analyst."

hammerhead sharks, and the rest of her toes, perhaps terrified of the killer big ones, cramped into tight curls and shied away. Corns spotted the knuckles, blisters broke out on her ankles, and callouses toughened the entire underside of her feet. Something about that pair suggested the abused child, the defeated soldier who had marched too long without boots. Rob refused to accompany Jude into a shoe store, afraid of what the salesmen thought. She wore nine and a half narrow, a forlorn, forsaken size. She wore, when she wasn't dancing, an anklet strung with tiny brass bells that sadly, continuously, tinkled. As she padded about the apartment Rob got the impression he was living with a little lost cat that shook its collar as it vainly searched for its home.

At first he was fascinated with those bells, but as time went by and he grew more content with the life he had chosen in New York, and more and more pleased with his paycheck, he sometimes grumbled about them. "Why don't you shed those superstitious slave chains?" he asked.

Jude stomped her foot. The very idea! "Jingle, ergo sum," she said.

The story of those bells, as it turned out, was the story behind that famous photograph. "You want to hear a good one?" Jude asked. "This is it." When she was seventeen, Judy Schitzman ("Geez, can you blame me for changing my name?") didn't want to visit Israel. She wanted to vacation in the Catskills or Atlantic City, like all the rest of the sacrilegious East Side kids. Such a curse! to have been adopted by an aunt and uncle so pious, so Old World, so anxious to talk of the hardships and narrow escapes. So committed to laying on the guilt. "Thick as cream cheese," Jude said.

Jude's own parents had met their tragic end when Ellen Schitzman knocked a plugged-in hairdryer into the bathtub, and Leo Schitzman, who found her electrocuted in the water, plunged his hand in. Even at age six, Jude was old enough to know she should be embarrassed by this farcical piece of history. When Uncle Chaim and Aunt Mina adopted her and placed her in a new school, she told her first-grade friends that her parents had been gassed in Poland. Her school chums seemed impressed.

"But you were born in 1950," Rob pointed out.

"So, was I good in math? And to a six-year-old, what's a little discrepancy in dates?"

To Chaim and Mina, it was everything. The nerve of her, making up such tales, making mockery out of one of the darkest hours in human history. So there hadn't been enough victims without Jude adding two more to the carnage? So there weren't enough horrors in the world without her fabricating more of them?

Chaim and Mina grated on Jude's nerves. "Two wet Yiddish rags," she said. They never let her tell a lie, and if you couldn't make things up, what was the point of living? Life, indeed, was boring. Jude knew if she wanted to be an artist she would have to pretend every minute was intense. She made it a point to rub everyone the wrong way. She purposefully aggravated her own sweet self. In front of a full-length mirror—Jude had always had her worst crises looking in a mirror—she hunched her shoulders and stuck her stomach out. "Judy Schitzman, you are one ugly mother," she whispered at her reflection. The next moment she gave herself a sultry smile and wink, sticking out her barely-there breasts. "Judy, dah-ling, how nice to see you! You look gohr-geous, absolutely rah-vishing, my dear."

Mina caught her in the schizophrenic act one day, and that's how Jude started ballet lessons. It was decided, in consultation with the rabbi, that Jude needed discipline. It was decided she had to get out of the house more, or Mina would have a nervous breakdown. "You'll have music lessons," Chaim told her. Jude stomped her feet. She couldn't stand still long enough to tune a violin. "French lessons," Mina suggested, and Jude howled. Bad enough she already mixed up Yiddish with English.

"I want belly-dancing lessons," she said.

"I'll teach you to dance," Chaim threatened. "I'll teach you to belly."

But in the end Jude was sent to a Russian ballet master, at quite a pretty penny. The ballet master was rude and ruthless. He spit orders in Jude's face as he turned out her arms, poked her in the gut, and practically yanked her head off her neck. He sneered at her. Curling his lip in disgust, he called her "Scheetzman." "Tuck in that belly, Scheetzman! Scheetzman, lower your chin, please! Scheetzman, I am going to snap that trunk of yours right in half!" Jude thoroughly enjoyed it. She liked the tap of his stick against the wooden floor; she liked being surrounded by mirrors. She loved throwing up, en masse, with all the other girls just before and after a lesson. She loved the Band-Aids and the Ace bandages and the injuries that made her cry. Ballet was wonderful—the music, the precision, the pain!

So Jude grew. She began to take modern dance because now she was too old to make it in the ballet world. Chaim and Mina were skeptical. Pink tutus were fine; nude leotards were not. Chaim was less and less willing to finance what he thought was an extravagant concession to the sexual revolution. Mina was worried about Jude catching splinters dancing in bare feet. Both were worried that Jude was obsessed with dance for all the wrong reasons. When Jude turned seventeen, Chaim and Mina decided it was time to break her of her fool ideas.

Jude was dragged to the sacred homeland, where everything and everybody got on her nerves. The Holy Land Hotel? How could it stack up to the Plaza? Esther Zeitz? Give her Bloomingdale's any day. The Biblical Zoo? Jude had seen bigger and better elephants in the Bronx. Israel was a disgusting, crummy old place. What was holy about all those stupid soldiers, about a land obsessed with its military?

Jude had never thought much about God before, but now her mind drifted toward more spiritual matters. She was sure God never lived inside a tank. God—at least Jude's God—was not a gun. God was Fifth Avenue at rush hour (furs and high heels and shopping bags from

Saks), Battery Park at twilight (Miss Liberty misty in the distance), and the top of the roof on Sunday morning. God was hot pastrami with a dab of horseradish on top. God was a great ballet. Jude leaned out of the hotel window in Jerusalem, dust and sweat gritted on her eyelashes. No wonder all those old guys in black were wailing at that dumb wall. Who wanted to live in the midst of a potential Armageddon, when you could live in glorious New York?

Judy Schitzman joined her aunt and uncle for breakfast in a street café. Chaim had rolls and coffee. Mina, on a perpetual diet that never seemed to work, confined herself to tea. Jude chowed down on eggs and rolls and coffee and juice, the eggs sticking suddenly in her throat when, halfway through breakfast, Chaim announced they would be making a permanent move to Israel before the year was up.

But Jude had to go back to New York. There was the dance studio. There was Central Park. There were hot dogs and pretzels and bagels. Fake suffering was great, to be sure, but she didn't want to really suffer in Israel. Jude threw down her fork on her plate. She wouldn't live in Jerusalem! She wouldn't join any old army! She looked horrible in khaki! What was she supposed to do for fun, go float in that stupid, smelly old Dead Sea? Besides, how could she dance in the middle of this cultural desert?

Chaim cursed. Jude could just lower her voice. Jude could just follow orders for once in her life. Jude could go straight to the dogs if she didn't like their plans. Mina, nervous from her tea, began to cry. Would there never be peace on earth? No, not as long as Jude was alive to fight with her uncle. Jude pushed back her chair. Where was she going? Her uncle had paid good money for that big breakfast. She had been eating them out of house and home for over ten years, and this was the thanks they should get? Besides, what about her parents? What about the past? She owed it to the past to live in Israel!

"I don't owe anybody anything," Jude said. "And you can drop dead!"

She fled the café. She stalked up a cobblestone hill, wandered down a side alley, and stumbled upon a street market. Such wonderful things for sale! Jude inspected them all, the colorful rugs and blankets, the pale yellow baskets, the sheer scarves, the heavy jewelry. In her purse she had all the money Chaim had given her before they left New York. She had planned to buy a new hot-pink leotard when she got back to the city, but now she resolved to spend every last cent on whatever would make her aunt and uncle most angry. Jude lingered before the stalls. Men eyed her. Men said things to her in languages she could not understand. She hesitated before she finally approached an Arab in long white robes. His dark face was shaded by a burnoose. His wares lay on a thick camel-colored blanket. Jude bent down. She fingered a heavy necklace, a collar that looked like something out of *Antony and Cleopatra*, before she finally grabbed what she thought was a bracelet strung with bells. It jingled. Yes, this was it. Something that made a Christmasy, goyish kind of noise.

When she stood up and tried to fasten it around her wrist, the Arab shook his head. He took the bracelet from her, bent down to the cobblestones, and clasped it around her ankle. Jude blushed, and pressed her cotton skirt against her thighs as the Arab eyed her legs. She backed away.

She gave him all the money in her purse down to the change. As she walked off, the tinkling of the bells above her sandals distinguished her from all the others on the street. Jude was pleased. She felt like a clown. She felt like a slave. See what Chaim and Mina would have to say about that! But within a minute she began to regret her decision, as if she had betrayed the aunt and uncle who had been kind enough to care for her almost all her life—and for an Arab, no less. She wanted her money back. The sounds of the bells made her feel sick.

She was at the top of the hill when she saw Chaim and Mina walking up towards her. Aunt Mina was out of breath; Chaim's face was red with rage. "You stay there!" he yelled. "You stay right there, young lady!" Jude wanted to run away. She wanted to run towards them and throw herself at their feet, but then they would see—and hear—the bells. So for once in her life, she obeyed. Chaim and Mina puffed up the hill. As Jude bent down to yank the bracelet off her ankle, light flashed, and then came the explosion. Glass and furniture and unidentifiable objects shattered out into the street. Jude ran down the hill toward the rubble. The bells jingled.

Mina was nowhere to be found. Chaim lay in two in the middle of the street, the skin of his right arm pale against the earth-colored cobblestones, ragged and bloody where it had been severed at the shoulder. His hand was turned palm upward, as if extended toward a cashier to receive some change. Jude didn't know what to do. She stooped down to touch the hand—it no longer was Chaim's hand—and ended up cradling the arm. The tiny digits tattooed there matched the numbers Jude had often observed on the arm of her uncle when he washed his hands before dinner or opened the stubborn lid on a jar of jelly.

When Rob asked her what she was thinking at the precise moment the photographer knelt down to shoot her, Jude considered it for a few seconds before she replied. "I felt excited, as if it weren't real, as if I were an actress in a show and any minute people would start applauding. I knew I would get my face in every magazine in America. It's awful—oh, I'm an awful person!—but I remember thinking, This is what I was born for, to be famous."

So five years later, ten years later, fifteen years later, Jude still had plenty to feel guilty about. "If only I were the type who wanted to live in Israel," she told Rob. "If only I had stayed at the breakfast table. If only I hadn't bought those bells. If only I had run down the hill a moment earlier. If only my parents hadn't died in the bathroom. If only I hadn't been born. If only I weren't Jewish!"

She loathed her history, and at the same time she felt superior to others because of it. "I like you," she told Rob, "and you've been lots of places and I guess you're kind of smart, but I mean, let's face it, your last name is Jones, you're so normal, so—so—adjusted" (Jude pronounced the last as if it were a dirty word), "so *American*. I mean, what do you people who aren't ethnic think about all day?"

"Sex and death," Rob said, "and taking a crap. Same as you, without the East Side accent."

But it was the accent that made her. Without it, who was Jude Silverman? The girl whose parents had fried in the bathtub? The girl whose aunt and uncle had been blown to pieces in an explosion? The girl who wore bells, the girl who danced "Hiroshima," the girl who was a bargain basement of neuroses, the girl who was a wholesale sack of bones, the girl in the bloody photograph, the girl in the mirror, staring sadly back? She wasn't anything, she wasn't anybody, without all that behind her. Chaim and Mina had been right. She owed something to the past, and she had known that intuitively, even way back when she had announced to her school chums that her parents had been sent to the gas chamber.

Rob, on the other hand, didn't owe anything. He lived for the here and now, for the action-filled moment. Jude was his link to the past, and Jude was his present, always responding so well to his camera. "Who'd you shoot today?" she asked when he came home, not bothering to listen to his reply. "Mmmm, photographer. Shoot me. I'm dying for it."

It was crazy. Jude was perverse. "Made for abuse," she whispered as she twisted into incredible positions Rob, except for one brief foray into pornographic photography, hardly knew existed. "Jude Silverman was built to last."

But she wasn't made to dance forever. Fifteen years after she had bought those bells, they were giving a muffled, melancholy jingle beneath the blankets every morning. "Oh God," Jude moaned, "why does anyone have to live past thirty?" Her back, once as supple as a roll of cookie dough, now felt as stiff as a cracker. Her knees creaked and complained. "Oh God, oh God, oh God," she moaned when she came home from a performance. "Oh God, rub my neck!"

Rob, with his skilled hands, filled in. "Ow!" Jude yelped when he pressed too hard. "What are you trying to do, kill me? I swear to God, everybody's out to get me. When I was waiting to cross Second this morning, a pigeon laid a number on me. When I was waiting to cross Park, a cabbie practically ran me over. So I decided the hell with this shit, I'll take the train. I went underground and the machine stole two of my tokens. I leaped over the turnstile, like a criminal on the run. Then I was waiting on the platform and this guy with a little black mustache looked like he was dying to push me on the tracks. So I walked down the platform and this punk came at me with purple hair and a T-shirt with a Nazi sign on it, you think I'm making this up? I said to myself, Jude Silverman, move those metatarsals. Run like bloody Mercury."

And now, the capper, what proved that the whole world was falling in on her: Jude Silverman, *the* Jude Silverman of "Hiroshima" fame, who had once brought down the house, was being relegated to just another member of the company corps. The Future/Dance/Theater was staging its own spectacular version of the end of the world, called, simply, "World War III," and Jude, who was hoping—expecting—to be chosen to dance the solo finale as the nuclear bomb, was doled out only a bit role as an intermediate-range ballistic missile. The nerve. It was an outrage!

Jude wailed. Rob tried his best to comfort her. "Look at it this way. If mighty empires can rise and fall and rise again, so can Jude Silverman."

"Mighty empires don't get sore feet. Mighty empires don't get arthritis. Mighty empires aren't Jewish. I'm a wash-up. There'll never be another World War III. It's over."

Jude planted her body in front of the mirror. She stuck out her tongue at herself and ran her fingers through her hair. She grabbed a pair of tweezers and went after her scalp. "I'm going to get every last gray one," she vowed. "I'm going to pull them all out. Search and destroy. This is Jude Silverman's mission."

"Pull out any more and you'll be bald," Rob warned.

Jude shrieked. "Whose head looks like a shiny pancake around here?"

"I can accept my age gracefully."

Jude stomped her feet and her bells jingled. "You were born an old man," she said. "I was born normal. I was born a baby. Look out. I'm getting ready to have a crisis. I'm having a crisis, I tell you."

Jude Silverman detonated. Meanwhile, "World War III," drawing highly favorable reviews, took New York by storm and raged on and on. The city was seized by an apocalyptic craze. The display windows at Macy's and Lord & Taylor's took on a futuristic cast, and a famous midtown jewelry store paid a special tribute to the war by placing five solitary diamonds in a blackened display case to represent stars glittering in a postnuclear sky.

"New York has gone berserk," Rob said. "I've never seen a city that so begs to be destroyed."

Jude took it too personally to care about the broader implications. "New York didn't do diddly squat for Hiroshima."

"Now Jude. Be reasonable. The apocalypse is in vogue. Hiroshima is like the Holocaust, totally passé."

"I told you. I'm a wash-up!" Jude's eyes filled with tears. "Let's have a wee one."

"An F-stop? Now?"

"You jerk! Nobody understands me! I mean, let's have a baby."

Rob stood shell-shocked. "In the middle of a world war? Where's your sense of social responsibility?"

"I never had any." Jude grabbed Rob. "Come on, photographer. Load your guns. Fire away."

Now who felt old? Rob's guns no longer worked on such short command. Besides, he wasn't prepared for this dilemma. He had been trained to keep his objective distance. He could more easily imagine photographing a nuclear bomb than he could snapping a shot of his own baby. A bomb, after all, was a bomb, but a baby was—well, uncertainty. He tried to persuade Jude. "It wouldn't be fair to bring a child into a world so deeply committed to destruction. A world of chemical warfare, Jude. A world of mass extermination."

Jude crossed her arms and looked unconvinced.

"Okay," Rob said, "how about a world where you have to push and shove in line just to get half a pound of pastrami?"

"Since when are you such a fan of pastrami?"

"All right, then. A world where people step on your feet on the subway and don't even apologize."

"Oh, so now it's manners that are going to save the world." Jude made a la-di-da face. "If only Hitler had read his Emily Post. Just think of the marvelous effect that would have had on the twentieth century. Pass the bombs, Fraulein. Pass the U-boats, mein Herr. Pass the soap, please. I say, Goering, not to bring up anything unpleasant, but doesn't it smell like gas in here?"

"Just put a stop to that," Rob said. "Just cut that out, Jude Schitzman, I mean, Silverman. Jesus Christ. You can't even make up your mind what your own name is. How are you going to raise a baby?"

"I want a baby," Jude said. "I want the blood and guts. I want the stink and the smell and the afterbirth. I want the baby to come out the way I should have come out, with the cord around its neck. I want to bleed to death on the operating table—"

Rob slapped her. Rob slapped Jude Silverman flat across the face and left a strapping red mark on her skinny cheek. He felt good. He felt satisfied. But he wasn't prepared for that reaction. He was prepared to apologize, until Jude smiled, infuriating him even more.

"You're neurotic," he said. "You're paranoid. You want to be hit. You beg for it. You're a bitch. You're a brat. I'll bet you were the worst kid on the block. I'll bet you were the worst kid ever born, period. You drove your parents to kill themselves. You drove your aunt and uncle crazy. You think you're so persecuted, but you do nothing but persecute everyone around you. I'm sick of your moaning and whining. You're a fraud. You're a compulsive liar. You're a basket case. I'll bet you bought those bells in Brooklyn. I'll bet you cut off your own uncle's arm with a butter knife."

"So what if I did?" Jude defended herself. "So what if that schmuck photographer told me exactly how to pose for him. He won that Nobel Prize, didn't he?"

"Pulitzer Prize! He won a Pulitzer for taking a fake shot of you, and here I am, stuck with the real, honest-to-goodness neurotic thing!"

"Oh!" Jude wailed. "You don't love me. You've never loved me, you only fell in love with my picture. Why'd you marry me? Why didn't you just let me kill myself?" She began to cry. "I hate photographers. I hate cameras. I hate myself in that picture."

Rob swallowed a lump in his throat. He felt guilt slide into his stomach. The feeling wasn't altogether unpleasant. He took the tearful Jude in his arms. "I never liked that picture," he lied. "You look so much better smiling. Come on now, say *cheese*. I'm sorry. I'm saying uncle, Jude."

Jude snuggled against him. "I'd like you better if you said *Daddy*."

Two months later, backstage at the Future/Dance/Theater, a giddy Jude Silverman, a buoyant Jude Silverman, paraded about with a pillow crammed down the front of her leotard, announcing to all who would listen, "Hey guys, I'm retiring, guess what for? It's called ending your career on a big bang—ha ha, get it? God, am I pregnant with wit, or what?" She smiled demurely, young-mother-to-be-ly. "I've always wanted a pair of tits," she mused. "The big guns. Real torpedoes."

Jude couldn't decide if she wanted a son or daughter. Rob thought twins would solve the problem, but Jude wasn't having any of it. "Too schizophrenic," she said. She placed her hands on her stomach. "Big Mama to control tower," she barked. "Do you read me? Come in."

She sighed and turned to Rob. "Big Mama is receiving neither masculine nor feminine vibes. Maybe it's a hermaphrodite. Maybe it's a
miscarriage. Maybe it's cancer. I'm sure it's cancer, Rob."

"Jude, it's a baby, take my word for it."

"Well. Okay. Let's call it Mordecai."

"Let's not."

Jude sighed. "Poor Morey. Just think of our genes waging war
within him, right at this very moment. Man, this is one time when I'm
willing to lose a fight." She put her hands back on her stomach. "Big
Mama to control tower," she barked again. "Do you read me? Life is
easier if you have blond hair."

She was growing calmer, and slightly dreamy. She was mooning
around the apartment all morning, and taking her stomach for long
walks in the afternoon. She was conspicuous now, for good reason: at
last, Jude Silverman was fat! Before, when people had stared at her,
she used to look fearfully back, but now she simply smiled and gazed
in equal wonder down at herself. "Guess what?" she told Rob. "I'm
less paranoid. But it's kind of boring. Jude Silverman could use a little
action."

"So take up knitting."

Jude, mildly, told him to shut up.

On her walks, she ate all the hot pretzels she wanted. She slurped
orangeade and lemonade and any other syrupy tutti-frutti drink she
could find. She thought, with fondness, of little Mordecai, and then
she thought of all the things that could go wrong. She was convinced,
for a while, that God would give her an unusual child, a deformed
little duck with three eyes and twelve toes, a freak, a weirdo, or a
saint. Her child would have to be different, at least from all those me-
diocre kids she saw on the street. She carefully inspected each one
that she passed. "Dumbo," she silently pronounced a droopy-eyed
toddler. "Pig," she labeled a little boy with the sticky residue of food
about his mouth. "Brat," she pegged a moaning girl who stomped her

feet. "If I ever had a kid like that, I'd strangle her." She smiled with
superiority, then jerked her head back to the little girl, finding a vague,
dissatisfying resemblance to herself. But her bad days were over now.
She sighed. She knew, in her heart of hearts, that she'd have a dull,
boring, well-adjusted child. It was guaranteed to be normal; with a
last name like Jones, how could it miss? It would yawn at the ballet
and laugh at her ostrich feathers. It would beg her to "take off those
embarrassing bells, Mo-therrr." After all the love and care she would
give it, it would turn on her, disown her, laugh at her, call her a kook.
This, then, would be all the thanks she would get!

Jude wrinkled her forehead. She was beginning to sound like Aunt
Mina. Maybe she was turning normal. Maybe she should worry.
Maybe she should walk all the way down Central Park. She made
a pilgrimage to Cleopatra's Needle and to the Alice in Wonderland
statue. She visited the carousel, where Chaim had taken her for rides
on the occasional Sunday, and where giggly, excited kids still lined up.

Jude walked away from the carousel and surfaced out of the park at
Temple Emanu-El. On Fifth, she heard chanting and rumbling. Hordes
of people clogged the sidewalk at 60th Street, marching straight up
the park. For a moment, Jude panicked. She almost took to her heels
and ran, but then she took her stomach in her hands and stood still,
as if preparing to be photographed. "Sit tight, Mordecai," she said.
"It's the Nazi invasion of midtown Manhattan. It's Armageddon, right
in our own backyard. Jude Silverman, Hebrew warrioress, proudly
stands her ground. Jude Silverman meets, with courage, her end!"

The crowd marched closer. They came upon her, bearing banners
of peace, not war, and Jude smiled to see their slogans were decorated
with serene little doves. *Bread, not bombs! No more Hiroshimas! No
more Nagasakis! Peace is at hand!* the signs said.

The crowd thronged the sidewalk. They carried banners that said
Catholics for Pacifism and *Muslims for Global Harmony*. They carried
banners in Hebrew characters Jude was ashamed she could no longer

understand. There were fresh-faced Hitler youth types carrying signs warning against the evils of _Die mutterrakete_. Jude loved the word. "Hey-hey, guys," she yelled and pointed to her stomach. "The mother rocket, that's me!"

The crowd passed by. Suddenly Jude felt overwhelmed. She felt sad. She walked back into the park and let her sense of smell lead her to the zoo. Colorful birds squawked at her, dirty farm animals bleated, and screaming monkeys put their paws over their eyes and ran away. "All right, you guys," Jude said. "I know where I'm not wanted." She jingled her way slowly to the polar bear's cage.

It was late summer, on the brink of fall. The leaves were beginning to crisp, and the wind picked up, while the sun beat down on the asphalt. It had been just this time of year when she was here with Rob, offering him a bite of that lousy pretzel that needed a dab of hot mustard on top. She'd been crying. And hadn't she, an hour before, threatened suicide? She seemed to remember a slight ruckus that afternoon. Rob had made fun of her black fishnet stockings. Rob had told her, joking around, she was the worst subject he had ever photographed—vain, stubborn, alternately belligerent as a rhinoceros and frightened as a little lamb. "Rhinoceros!" Jude said. "I don't like the smell of that, Rob Jones. What are you, some kind of closet anti-Semite?"

"I said rhinoceros because . . . Jude, what the hell are you doing, changing the curtains?"

"The whole world is out to kill Jude Silverman. Well, Jude Silverman will show the world a thing or two. Jude will kill herself!"

"Now Jude. Don't do that."

"I was born to die."

"Yes, but you can do it later."

Now it was later, and she was too tired to think of suicide. Jude finally made her way to the polar bear cage. She sat down on a park bench and watched the dirty, shaggy beast who, years after that scene with Rob, still paced his cage, like a madman, back and forth. He seemed so wild-eyed, so out of control. "Settle down now, you smelly old bear," she said. Then she smiled. "Come on out of that cage, you chicken shit. Maul me. Strangle me. Break my bells. Just don't harm my little Mordecai, is that a deal?" The polar bear panted and ignored her. Jude sleepily, deliciously, rested her hands upon her stomach and closed her eyes. The past? Just a bugaboo, compared to the future threatening to detonate inside her. It sure took a lot of strength to keep on living, Jude thought, finally feeling, kicking within her, what little energy she needed to survive.

Lifelines

The spring I worked in the Dairy Queen I hated everything: school and home and work, my teachers, my manager, my mother, myself. I was always walking toward something, always waiting for something wonderful to happen, waiting for a card or letter from my father, waiting for love to strike. But I bumped into more things than I consciously found, and I lost things habitually. Either I was shedding or I had bad luck. In any case, I lost two sets of house keys that spring, and every other day before I walked to work I lost a quarter in the school Coke machine. I lost so many quarters I went to our principal, Mother Superior, and complained.

"If you lose something, you ought to know what to do," she said, gazing down at me through her silver half-glasses.

"Go look for it?" I said.

"Wrong. Pray to Saint Anthony. He has divine intercession and can find you anything."

My mother snorted when I told her what Mother Superior had said. "Can the great saint find me my lost youth?" she said. "And can he find me a man? That's what I want to know. I'd believe in saints if I could see miracles like that."

My mother was old at thirty-five, and looked worn out. I was seventeen and I didn't believe in saints either. I didn't believe anything lost could ever be found, at least not in its original state. Still, I wanted to grab onto things, seize them, get whatever I could get, even if I couldn't hang on to them.

Wanting steady things to surround me came from moving place to place. My father worked construction, and we moved up and down the coast, following the jobs. For every place we lived I found a special shell on the beach. "Why do you want to carry those broken shells around with you?" my father asked.

"They wouldn't get broken if we didn't move so much," my mother commented before I could even answer.

"If we didn't move so much, she wouldn't have the chance to find them in the first place," my father said.

"If we didn't move so much and everything else wasn't so topsy-turvy, she wouldn't want to collect them," my mother said.

"You think everything's topsy-turvy?" my father shouted. "I'll show you topsy-turvy, my friend."

"Nothing's the way it used to be!" my mother said.

"It's always been the same, no matter where we moved: lousy, lousy, and lousy again."

"If it's so lousy," my mother said, "then get out."

My father got out. My mother chose Port Charlotte, sight unseen, for the name. "It's not a *beach,*" she said scornfully. "It's not a *fort,* it's a port, and it's Port Charlotte. Charlotte, Charlotte—doesn't that name sound good and old-fashioned? Comforting?"

My manager at the Dairy Queen, Bob, said it sounded like the name of a Southern belle withering away on a sagging front porch. "Charlotte sounds like the name of some old maid saving herself up for some Prince Charming. Charlotte's wasting her whole life waiting for the prince to come along when there's somebody else just as good waiting on the front porch next door. She's a dying flower, that Charlotte girl." He winked at me.

I thought about my mother, shuffling around the house until noon on a Saturday in her slippers and thin, see-through nightie. When I told her to get dressed, she said, "I'm not going anywhere, so what's the point?"

Bob was as old as my mother, but he was more like my father. "I'm an enterprising fellow," he said one afternoon as he stood by the chocolate syrup machine. "I don't let anything stand in the way of what I want to get. You look like you're having a little trouble tying on that apron, Mary Ellen."

"I can get it myself," I said.

I didn't tell my mother that Bob and I worked the afternoon shift at the Dairy Queen alone. She would have disapproved. I was always careful to complain just the right amount about my job at home, but awful as it was, I sometimes looked forward to it. Bob and I usually worked without talking for the busy first hour. We bumped into each other sometimes as we backed away from the counters. The bit of Coke left in the can I finally had coaxed out of the fickle school vending machine tasted warm and flat, but familiar and good, and even though I watched it every day through the tall windows of the Dairy Queen front, there still was mystery in the way the Port Charlotte sky grew dark in the afternoon, and clouded over. Bob and I had made up a game called the Rain Game. Each person tried to predict the exact moment the storm clouds would break and pour down rain. The person who guessed closest to the minute won the right to sit down, while the other person had to serve the winner a miniature hot fudge sundae.

"Four-thirty," Bob predicted.

"Quarter to five, quarter to five," I sang. I felt smug when the hands of the clock edged past four-thirty and the sky turned pitch.

The first clap of thunder shook the building at 4:46, emptying the parking lot and reducing the music on the radio to static. Bob switched it off. He grumbled as he held the plastic dish of ice cream under the chocolate syrup spigot. "You're a smartass," he said, "but you're my best girl. And you know why?" He winked at me. " 'Cause you know who's boss around here."

"And who might that be?" I asked.

"Well, I've heard he's really smart and really good-looking," he said. "His name's B-O-B."

I shrugged. He laughed and handed me my miniature chocolate sundae.

Outside, the rain came sheeting down the tall windows. Bob pulled up a stool beside me. "Your skin's too pale," he said.

"So what."

"So nothing. It just means you probably don't get enough sun and fun. You like to have a little fun, I bet."

"I guess," I said. I kept on eating. The hot fudge was sickly sweet and I dug deep with my white plastic spoon to bring up the vanilla ice cream.

"Like right now," he said. "There aren't any customers, so we ought to have a little fun, Mary Ellen, just you and me."

"What's your idea of fun?"

"What's yours?"

"We could play a guessing game," I said.

"Go on, guessing games."

"They're fun if you try to guess the right things."

"Like what?"

"Like the kind of things you wouldn't find out about people in ordinary conversations. Things that tell you something about the other person, like what they wanted to be when they were little, and stuff like that," I said.

"Who cares about what people wanted to be when they were little?"

"It tells a lot about them as grown-ups."

"Yeah, well, I forgot what I wanted to be," Bob said. "Anyway, I never turned into it." He sighed. He rubbed his hands back and forth over the stains on the thighs of his uniform pants. "Stop looking at me that way," he said.

"I'm not looking at you."

"It isn't the past that counts, anyway. It's the future."

"I guess."

"The Rain Game's enough of guessing games."

The chocolate syrup machine buzzed. The buzz died into a hum. Bob rubbed his hands together. "Time to get serious."

I thought he was going to suggest cleaning the counters. Instead, he examined his thumbnail, then suddenly looked up. "You like to read palms?" he asked.

"Psalms?"

"No, palms, p-a-l-m-s. Tell fortunes."

"I've never done it," I said.

"What do you mean, never? I thought that's what girls do at slumber parties. Sit around in their pajamas, talk about boys, curl their hair, read palms and jazz like that."

"If you're Catholic, telling the future is a sin."

"You gotta be kidding!" he said.

"I'm not."

"But don't they teach you that God's got it all figured out before it happens?"

"Sure."

"So don't you figure you got as much right as God to know what sort of things are going to happen to you?"

"I guess."

"It isn't God who's got to live your life."

"That's true," I said. "It's me."

"Isn't God who's got to get up and go to work every morning. Isn't God who's got to tell customers yessir and no ma'am. So why don't you put that sundae down," he said, taking it out of my hands. I watched him set it on the counter with regret. "Let's do a little palm-reading, a little fortune-telling, while there aren't any customers." He looked at me expectantly. I held out my left hand. He cleared his throat, moved his stool up closer, grinned, and took my hand. Chocolate syrup clogged his short fingernails; a smear of vanilla ice cream crossed the top of his hand. He turned my palm upwards and traced his finger across it. The skin on the tip of his finger was rough. Underneath my hand, on his hand, I could feel his callouses.

"This is the Lifeline," he said. "It tells you how long you're going to live."

"Don't tell me," I said. "I'm afraid to die."

He snapped his chewing gum and leaned closer. "Then I'm happy to report you're going to live a long and healthy life. But every break in the Lifeline—here, here, and here, man, you got a lot of them—..eans something traumatic is going to happen. Something B-I-G that's going to change your whole life. Now you're born here—" He jabbed his finger halfway between my thumb and index finger. "And then here's the first break less than a fourth of the way up your hand. So calculating you're about seventeen or so, I'll bet the first traumatic thing has already happened, might I be right?"

I nodded.

"And it seems to me the way this line moves—" Bob scratched his head. "I don't know, something about it—means it's got something to do with your parents."

I nodded.

"The line kind of splits and breaks off into two here. Your parents divorced?"

"So what?" I said. "Lots of people's parents are."

"Did I say anything moralistic?"

"That isn't a word," I said.

"You got a dictionary in your back pocket, Smartypants?"

"Nope."

He laughed. "You live with your mother?"

I nodded.

"Father left your mother, huh? For some other person, maybe, of the female sexaroo? Some lady friend?"

"What's it to you?" I said.

"It's all in the lines, you see. You see how this stronger line, this masculine line, breaks off? See how it intersections with this weaker line here, while the other, weaker line—meaning of the female sex— just wanders off on its lonesome without intersectioning with any- thing?"

"Inter*sect*ing."

"Intersecting, intersectioning, what's the difference? Either way your father gets the woman while your mother doesn't get anything."

I tried to pull my hand back, but Bob hung onto it. He looked me straight in the eye. Then he drew his stool closer with his left hand. The rain beat against the windows. Outside, in the parking lot, a palm frond ripped slowly off its trunk and fell like a feather onto the asphalt.

"So then your Lifeline continues," Bob said. "Because even though you thought maybe you would die when your father packed his bags and left you, you kept on living. And your mother, she kept on living too, right?" He cleared his throat, squinted his eyes, and concentrated on my palm. "But enough of that. Now you got yourself a Lifeline, and then, Mary Ellen, you got yourself a Loveline. You consult your Loveline to find out all about the loves of your life and whether or not you're going to win or lose at them. The Loveline, see, starts right up where the Lifeline begins. That means the closest love in your life is the love you got for your parents, and you can't get away from that, ever."

I nodded.

"Okay, so then after that comes the first crack in your Loveline. Quit turning all red there."

"I'm not turning red."

"You know what that means, I guess."

"It doesn't mean anything."

"It means enough to make your face turn red."

I pulled my hand away. One of his nails scraped the length of my pinkie finger. "It doesn't mean anything, because I don't believe in any of it."

"You think I was just making it up as I went along?"

"Yes."

He leaned closer to me and took my hand back. "So what's the matter, you don't admire a guy with a little imagination?"

I shook my head.

He let go of my hand. I turned my head so I didn't have to look at him. Outside, in the rain, a couple pulled up in a red Buick and ran up to the counter, holding hands and laughing. Bob jerked his head toward the counter and headed back to the coat room. "Looks like you have yourself a customer, Mary Ellen," he said.

I stood, and hesitated a little, the way I always hesitated when I stood up from the sand after lying too long in the sun on the beach. The couple knocked on the service window. They knocked again, and I went over and yanked open the glass. Hot, humid air hit my face. The rain splashed down on the asphalt.

They wanted banana splits. They wanted just a little syrup on the ice cream, the bananas cut up teeny-weeny, and heavy on the nuts on top. My hands felt funny. My fingers tingled and went numb. I clutched the dishes too hard and the wax coating flaked off underneath my nails. I was afraid I would drop the dishes.

"Not so much whipped cream," the man called out.

Bob came out of the coat room. "Give the customers what they want," he said.

The whipped cream piled up on the dish. I moved over to the chocolate syrup spigot. I put too much pressure on it, and syrup pooled up on top.

"Mary Ellen," Bob said. "Hey, Mary Ellen, what the hell are you doing? You heard the customer! Give the customer what he wants!"

He grabbed the dish away from me and threw it in the trash can, where it hit the bottom with a thud. "You're good for nothing," Bob said, making up two more banana splits. "Just goes to show you if you want something done right, do it yourself."

The couple at the window snickered. I turned my face away from the glass so they wouldn't see me.

"And how many times do I have to tell you to close the service window?" Bob hollered, after the customers drove off. "You think we get our AC free?"

I untied my apron fifteen minutes early. Bob followed me into the coat room. "You taking off before the buzzer?" he asked, his voice apologetic. "Don't forget to punch out before you leave." As I pushed the back door to the parking lot, I heard him calling, "Hey, you're supposed to punch out, company regulation! And besides, your shift ends at six!"

I looked back and saw him standing in the doorway, hands on his hips, towel draped over his wrist. He waved. I walked away.

The rain had stopped as abruptly as it had started, but the air was still muggy. The traffic had cleared off Old Washington Road, but the sidewalks were cluttered with soggy pine cones, palm branches downed in the wind, and long, flesh-colored earthworms edging onto the cement off the grass. I gazed into the windows of the shops I passed: Quinlan's Grocery, where the drawers of the cash register were left open to prove to thieves they were empty, Miss Desiree's Salon of Beauty, where the chairs tilted at odd angles away from the mirrors, as if never expecting to be sat upon again.

No lights shone through the windows of the apartment, but because I was in the habit of lifting the top of the mailbox as quietly as if I were stealing something from it, I lifted it just as softly as I would have had my mother been waiting, and listening, on the other side of the door. Nothing inside. My mother was right; I looked in there too often. "So he sent you a birthday card," she told me last week. "You'd be a damn sight better off if he sent the alimony check."

I stood on the outside steps of the apartment, unlocked the door, and reached in to turn on the hall light. I closed my eyes and gave the cockroaches time to climb into the woodwork before I went in. I turned the box fan on high, lit the stove, and shoved some frozen fish filets under the broiler. I changed into a T-shirt and shorts, and combed my long, scraggly hair. I was staring in the hall mirror, thinking *Someone just made a pass at me,* when my mother let the screen door slam.

I turned. But I couldn't look her flush in the face because I was afraid she might know what I had been thinking. She wore her white blouse and red skirt and the red criss-crossed sandals with the bright gold buckles. Her toenails were supposed to be painted to match the sandals, but the polish was too orangey to match the red. She carried a paper bag. "This is for you," she said. "And I'm sorry I couldn't give it to you on your birthday, but I didn't have enough cash to take it off layaway."

The paper bag fell to the linoleum as she pulled out and held up a white blouse which was a slight variation on the one she wore: sleeveless polyester, with a wide collar turned back into a V-neck, the breast pocket cut and stitched to resemble eyelet. I never had liked the blouse she wore, any more than I liked her red criss-crossed sandals, but once or twice I had told her she looked nice in it because I wanted to make her feel pretty. But she wasn't pretty. She wasn't vibrant, like my father's wife, Janine. Janine was my idol. "You're my candle on a dark night," my father once said to her, hugging her. Janine would never wear a sad-sack blouse like that.

"That's just like yours," I told my mother. The disappointment must have seeped into my voice; she dropped her arms and the blouse fell in her hands like a limp rag.

"I can't return it," she said. "I bought it on sale."

I reached out and touched the fabric. "It's really pretty," I forced myself to say. "And yours looks so nice on you."

"Try it on," she said. "See how it fits."

I turned my back to her and pulled my T-shirt over my head.

"Why don't you wear your bra?" she asked.

"It's too hot."

"You'll sag before you're twenty."

I turned around only enough to take the blouse from her. I slipped it over my head. She put her hands on my shoulders as if she were afraid I might bolt away before I looked in the hall mirror. Her hands were so much more gentle than Bob's; they used so much less force, but were still persuasive. But I didn't want to be persuaded. I didn't like Bob or my mother or the blouse, which hung down past my waist, covering my shorts. On the side of the blouse without the pocket, the dark outline of my nipple showed through the thin material. I looked naked.

"You look—very pretty," my mother said. I knew she meant it no more than I had meant it the one or two times I had told her the same thing. I shivered when I felt her warm breath tickling the hairs on my neck.

"Any boys yet?" she asked softly.

I thought of Bob. I thought of my father. "No," I said.

"People don't appreciate," she said. "Nobody appreciates what you have inside. It's all what you look like. It's all how well you can pass off being happy when really you're miserable inside." She sighed. "That Janine," she said. "Janine, Janine—doesn't that just sound like the name of some slut?"

"It does not."

"Whose side are you on?"

"Nobody's. I'm not on anybody's side."

"You could have fooled me," she said. Her fingers closed tighter around my arm. "Don't ever let me hear about you carrying on with any boys."

"I'm not."

"That's just the kind of thing your father would encourage."

"He would not!"

"They're all after one thing. And then they call you a tease, and worse, if you don't give them what they're after." She let go of my arm and inhaled deeply. "What's that smell?" she asked. She walked into the kitchen. I rubbed my arm. I heard her yank the stove open. I smelled the fish filets crisping.

She came into the doorway. "I tell you time and time again, and still you don't listen. You don't listen—you don't listen! How many times do I have to tell you it's better to slow-cook something in the oven than burn it under the broiler?"

She was sleeping on the couch as I turned off the lights that night. The Lifeline couldn't register the small, horrible things that happened, like hearing your mother snore. It couldn't register the rustle of a cockroach exploring the inside of the paper bag my mother had left lying on the linoleum. Naked in front of the bathroom sink, I scraped my nails across a wet bar of soap, then took a metal nail file and pushed all the soap out. I couldn't get my hands clean enough.

The End of the Season

Rich was putting on the pressure. Two months had gone by since my father died, and I still hadn't decided what to do with the house. With the sort of resolution that made him so successful at business, Rich sat me down with a pencil and paper and made me list all the negative and positive aspects of the place. Under the minus sign I accumulated *too old, falling apart, ugly carpets, ugly wallpaper, radiators hiss like snakes, already have our town house, bad memories,* and *I hate Cold Creek.* Then I stared at the plus sign for half a minute. "Well," Rich said, "what about the big backyard? The front porch? All the bedrooms? And the den?"

I chewed on the pencil eraser. Rich sighed, folded the list into a paper airplane, and shot it across the room, where it nose-dived into the TV. "Take Friday off," he said. "Whether we sell it or keep it, we still need to clean out the place."

So Friday found me back in my old bedroom, rooting through the strange array of stuff I had abandoned when I left home for college at seventeen. Among the oddities I came across were a foot-long piece of fishing wire half strung with tiny purple and orange beads, a tin of all-natural strawberry lip gloss in which the sticky corpse of an ant was embalmed, a vial of aromatic musk oil that gave me a headache, and a tarnished POW bracelet bent in an oval so tight it reminded me of how stick-skinny my wrists once had been. I forced the bracelet onto my right wrist and went across the hall.

Rich was rummaging deep in the crawl space off my parents' old bedroom. On the carpet lay box upon box of Christmas ornaments, a needlepoint footstool with a broken leg, and a transparent plastic bag full of dolls, their arms in rigid position at their sides, their eyes open in wonder, and their shiny, smooth buttocks revealed by the disarray of their skirts. In the corner, Rich had set aside the musical rocking chair I'd sat in when I was no bigger than a doll myself. I went over and touched the back of the chair. As it tipped back and forth, "Rock-A-Bye Baby" played. The tune sounded tinny and worn down. I grabbed the arm of the chair and stopped the music.

"Get a load of this," I called. Rich came out of the crawl space, his shoulders hunched and his hand supporting his lower back. A gray smear of dust ran the length of his right cheek, and his sandy hair, which badly needed to be cut, was frizzed above his ear and streaked with a long cobweb.

"Remember these?" I asked, holding out my wrist.

"Sure," he said. "I had one."

"I wonder what happened to old Private First Class William Redman."

Rich took my wrist in his hand. He blinked when he saw the inscription. "He never came back."

"How do you know?"

He shrugged. "Adrienne had that same bracelet. She checked into it."

Adrienne was the girl Rich had been in love with in college. *Head over heels,* he once admitted to me. *And I mean in that sick way, when you would do anything.* I knew. I'd had one of those myself, with a British guy named, of all things, Hugo Titley. I'd been crazy for him, so crazy that when I realized he wasn't as wild about me I left out my diaphragm and got pregnant, hoping that would prove the strength of my devotion. But all it ended up proving was the weakness of his. Hugo went back to England and I went through with the abortion. It was legal by then.

With one finger I traced William Redman's name on the bracelet. "I
guess I didn't really care about this guy," I said. "I mean, I wrote my
letters to Congress, asking them to investigate his case, and then . . .
I don't know. I just dropped it."

"You couldn't have brought him back."

"I could have written more letters."

"It was just a fad, like everything else was then."

"Not to this guy's family."

Rich was losing patience. "You weren't part of his family," he
pointed out. He looked down at the boxes piled on the carpet and then
looked back into the crawl space. "Christ, look at all this stuff."

"Let's break for a beer," I said.

Rich took off his glasses and rubbed his eyes. I was always surprised, when he did that, to discover how much his glasses worked to
camouflage his age, to hide the wrinkles at the sides of his eyes, the
dark circles underneath, and the few white hairs that had popped up
recently in his eyebrows. He flicked a speck of dust off the lens, then
put his glasses back on. "I need to wash up," he said.

I went downstairs, squeezing the bracelet tighter around my wrist
and brooding about something I couldn't quite identify. Staring into
the refrigerator, which was empty except for a small box of baking
soda and the six-pack we had brought to help us through the afternoon, I thought about how one era of my life was over and another
had long since begun. Maybe another one was beginning. I heard the
tinny music of the rocking chair playing inside my head. To block
it out, I opened drawer after drawer noisily, in search of the bottle
opener. After I finally found it, in a drawer full of miscellaneous junk,
I opened two of the beers, telling myself to calm down. Just because
Dad was dead, I thought, didn't mean everything else had to change.
But everything already seemed different—fragile and scary.

My mother had died so neatly, so silently I could almost convince
myself an angel had descended and whisked her away in her sleep. But
Dad went so slowly, so untidily, so viscerally I couldn't romanticize

it. I had to help him change his colostomy bag. I had to watch him
sign an organ donation form as he lay in the hospital bed. "I guess
they want the eyes," Dad said, as he peered down at the form through
his reading glasses, "and maybe the liver or the kidneys. They won't
want those bowels of mine, that's for darn tootin'."

The way he willed his body away absolutely chilled me. "Well,
what do you expect him to do?" Rich asked me later when I told him
about it.

"I want him to fight back."

"He *has* fought back."

I knew it was selfish, but I wanted him to fight even more—not so
much for himself, but for me.

I took a long drink of my beer. Rich came downstairs, one hand on
the banister and one hand on the small of his back. He had rubbed his
face too hard with the towel; behind his glasses, his eyebrows looked
crooked, and the skin on his cheeks was too pink. "Massage tonight?"
he asked.

"Sure thing, old man."

Rich groaned and took the beer from me. "Wrong thing to say,
Janie."

"Sorry," I said.

Out on the front porch, it was warm and sunny. Most of the leaves
were still on the trees, but they were beginning to dry and curl at the
edges, and some had already fallen, still green, to the ground. A few
squirrels nervously searched the front lawn for acorns. We sat on the
steps and watched them.

"It's the end of summer," I said, sadly.

"But it's the beginning of fall," Rich said.

"I hate fall."

"Don't you like the leaves? And wearing sweaters? Come on. I
know you like to snuggle underneath the blankets in bed."

"I hate the change of seasons," I said.

Either fed up or mystified by my moodiness, Rich shrugged. We fell silent, drank our beers, and watched the occasional car go by, until a yellow school bus pulled up across the street.

The bus ride didn't seem to have changed much since I was a student at Cold Creek High. The boys still sat one to a seat in the back of the bus, while in the front the girls sat in whispery, giggly pairs. In the middle of the bus one girl sat by herself, her forehead pressed against the window, her lower lip heavy, and her eyes glazed as she stared at Rich and me. I knew she wasn't registering what she saw. Her mind was probably on some bad grade she'd gotten, a recent humiliation suffered in gym class, or her failure to make the lead in the school play. Maybe she was dreaming of a boy she liked who would never like her back. Or maybe she was scheming to run away from her parents and everyone else in Cold Creek.

Her sad, lonely face bothered me. I was glad when the bus pulled away. The group of kids left on the sidewalk split up and straggled down the street in opposite directions, the girls clutching their books to their half-formed breasts, the boys carelessly holding them in one hand by their side. A couple of the boys, knocking into one another, started to scuffle. "Eat shit, man," one called out. "Suck off, faggot," the other answered. "Lap pussy."

Rich and I looked at one another, laughed nervously, then looked away. "Is there anything worse than a teenage boy?" I asked. "Besides a teenage girl?"

Rich stared at the spot on the step where the red paint had chipped off, revealing the gray cement underneath. "I was completely out of control of myself when I was that age," he said.

"What was the worst thing you ever did?" I asked.

He hesitated a moment and picked a dust ball off the cuff of his workshirt. "I broke into the girls' lav with a bunch of guys. After hours. With a Magic Marker."

"And?"

"Well. Use your imagination."

I laughed. "Pricks, drawn six feet high on the walls. For a good time, call *blank,* and you inserted the principal's name."

"Something like that." Rich took a swallow of his beer and wiped his mouth with the back of his hand. "My parents grounded me for six weeks."

"I was rotten to my parents when I was growing up," I said.

"Dad said you were a real hell-raiser," Rich said.

It never used to bother me when Rich called my father Dad—I thought it was nice of him to show my father affection—until one day in the hospital Dad happened to introduce us to a nurse we'd seen there often. "This is my daughter and son-in-law," Dad said proudly, and the nurse said, "Oh, I thought you two were brother and sister!" That had irked me to no end. I wondered if that was the way other people perceived me and Rich, as a couple of familiar old siblings.

"I wasn't a hell-raiser," I said. "Dad just got all bent out of shape about Hugo."

"I'd get bent out of shape too if my daughter was going out with a Neanderthal man in Birkenstocks."

I had always regretted showing Rich a picture of Hugo. Rich had peered at the photo for a full moment, taking in Hugo's full beard and long hair and the beads around his neck, before he said, "Nice dashiki."

"I don't know what Mom and Dad expected when they met Hugo," I said. "In any case, they totally overreacted to him. Mom pursed her lips the minute I brought him up the front steps, and Dad wouldn't even look at him. The only typically British thing he did was call me 'love' every other second. The worst thing he did was make fun of the royal family and defend the IRA."

"Your parents must have flipped."

"Mom kept asking me about the status of Hugo's visa. Once she even said American girls were all suckers for ethnics. Then Dad kept on mispronouncing Hugo's name."

"They must have been relieved when you two broke up."

"Actually, we got along even worse after that," I said. "The weekend after he left, I went home. I looked like a mess. I hadn't slept right for days. But I hadn't told my parents anything, so the first thing Dad asked me when I got in the door was 'So, Janie, what news of our friend Who-go?'"

Rich laughed.

"I went off my nut. I kept hollering 'Hew-go, Hew-go, Hew-go!' and I screamed that Hugo was gone, but he would have been with me at that very minute if only my anti-intellectual, pro-establishment bourgeois father had learned how to pronounce his name right."

"Weak argument."

"I know," I said. "But I had to blame somebody."

"So why did you blame Dad? He was just acting the way any other father would."

"Whose side are you on, anyway?"

"I'm not sure," Rich said. "Tell me what Dad said."

"Oh, you know," I said. "The old parental song and dance. That I was a phony and Hugo was a fake. That the reason we were so committed to the poor and the hungry and the oppressed was because we were scared to death of making a real commitment to each other." I fell silent for a moment. I could almost hear my father's voice ringing in my ear. " 'You kids want excitement,' he said, 'you want dramatics, you want to care more about some missing soldier in Vietnam, some black man from Mississippi you've never even met, than you want to care about your own mother and father. You never visit us, you never write, and when you're here you can't be bothered giving your aunts and uncles the time of day. Let me tell you something, kiddo,' he said. 'Charity begins at home, right here in your own backyard. When are you going to grow up and realize it?' "

"That sounds like Dad all right," Rich said.

"God, I hated him for saying that."

"I always hated it when my parents were right, too."

"So you *are* on his side?"

"It's a dead issue," Rich said. "I mean, let's face it, our generation did grow up pretty late."

"What do you mean 'late'?"

"Oh, you know," he said. "Settling down. Getting married."

I shrugged. Rich laughed and patted me on the back. Resting his elbows on his knees, he held the mouth of the bottle in one hand and tilted the bottle back and forth. "Think your father ever guessed you had an abortion?"

I shook my head.

"Just as well, I'm sure."

"How do you think he would have reacted?" I asked.

Rich raised his eyebrows. "He was your father, Janie."

"But I'd like to know what you think," I said.

Rich deliberated for a moment. "I think that would have hurt him more than anything."

"I wouldn't be too sure of that," I said.

I closed my eyes. I had a secret. That fight I'd had with my father with Hugo was nothing compared to the one I'd had with him about Rich. It happened the morning I drove Dad back from the hospital, before we were certain he had cancer. I'd taken him in for a diagnostic test, a barium enema that the radiologist told us would last, at most, only thirty minutes, but which ended up taking over two hours. For some reason—maybe it was fright, or maybe old age had loosened his sphincter muscles—Dad couldn't hold the barium they injected into his colon. He kept expelling it on the examining table before the radiologist could track its movement on the X-ray. Each time he expelled it, they had to inject it all over again, until Dad finally was able to control himself and they completed the test.

As I drove him home, he described the enema as something only the devil himself could have invented. As he laughed weakly to cover his embarrassment, soft, bubbly noises came from inside his pants. His face turned red. "I'll pull over," I said.

He shook his head. "Unless you're worried about the car seat?"

"No, not at all," I said. He hadn't been allowed solid food for the previous two days, so it was only the barium that he was losing.

He touched the dashboard. "I wouldn't want to ruin Rich's car."

"It's my car, too," I said, annoyed because he always seemed to assume we paid for everything with Rich's salary, not mine. "You know Rich wouldn't care anyway."

"He'd understand," Dad said. "He'll have a good laugh tonight when we tell him what I've been through."

"Rich won't laugh."

"Sure he will," my father said, and the sound of the barium erupted again as if to prove it. I tried to concentrate on driving. I tried not to listen to the noises and tried not to think my father might have cancer. But I couldn't stop myself from wondering if this was the beginning of a long, slow end, from imagining how awkward I would feel when Dad told me he was going to die, and the embarrassment we would feel when we realized we had an obligation to tell each other something we both felt but had never expressed. I couldn't imagine telling my father "I love you." Just thinking of it made me uncomfortable and made me not want to look over at Dad, who was staring out the window, probably thinking the same thoughts, too. Then I knew we wouldn't have to wait for the test results to come back. It wouldn't even matter if they were positive or negative; what mattered most was that at that moment we both had faced the fact that he was going to die, sometime soon or in the future, and we had to acknowledge it.

"I'd like to tell you something," my father said.

"Don't, Dad," I said, squinching my eyes together and blinking. "Not while I'm driving."

"No, let me say my piece," he said. I tightened my hands on the steering wheel, tensed for what was going to come, but relieved that he had taken the first step towards saying it. He cleared his throat.

"I've never told you," he said, "that I think Rich is good for you. I think Rich was a good choice."

I stared through the windshield. My eyes stung. The median blurred; trees and signs flashed by. I thought, bitterly, about how my father and I never seemed to connect.

"What does Rich have to do with any of this?" I asked. I should have stopped there, but I kept on going. "And what does 'good choice' mean? That Rich is a great guy because he makes a lot of money?"

I looked over at Dad. He looked confused. "I meant he's a good man. All those other ones—they weren't right for you, Janie."

My voice went up a pitch. "Why weren't they right for me?"

"They weren't interested in the right things."

"Like what? Settling down? Having a job? Buying a house? Having kids?"

Even though that was exactly what he meant, my father, hearing scorn in my voice, wasn't going to admit it. "What did I say?" he asked. "I said one thing—you married a decent man."

"All right," I said, hoping he would drop the subject. But he kept on going, listing all of Rich's attributes, as if it was a Kiwanis Club dinner and he was introducing Rich as the honored guest. How Rich was responsible. How he brought home the dough. How he knew the value of the dollar. How he was always there when my father needed his help, how he was willing to shovel the walk and mow the lawn, how he was polite to my aunts even though some of them ranked among the most difficult women alive. How he was good to me, and took me out to dinner once a week, and on vacation twice a year, and helped out around the house. I was the luckiest girl in the world. I couldn't have asked for better.

"That's some speech of praise," I said. "Too bad you left the most important thing out."

"What's that?" Dad asked.

I thought about my mother and father, about how they had existed for years in the same house, living not like man and wife, but like a couple of amicable boarders. "You didn't say he loved me," I said.

"You have to hear that from me?" he asked.

I pressed my lips together. They were dry and flaky because I'd been licking them nervously while my father was undergoing the barium enema. "Forget it," I said. "I'm glad you like Rich. I like him too."

My father turned his head and looked out the window. All the way home I kept my lips pressed resolutely together, as if to deny I was wavering between feeling sorry for my father (he meant well, he deserved better, I'd been incredibly cruel to him on what probably had been one of the most difficult and humiliating mornings of his life) and feeling an inexplicable, irrational hatred for him, for being old, for saddling me with the burden of his sickness, for reminding me of the indignity of old age, for touching on a sore spot inside me and making me realize there was a big difference between love and like, and making me wonder, once again, where Rich and I fell on that broad spectrum.

I never told Rich about that conversation I had about him with my father. There wasn't any point in hurting him. But what kept me from hurting him? I wondered. Was it love, or just a feeling of decency, of obligation to do right by him because he was my husband? I couldn't decide. When I doubted the way I felt about Rich, it was convenient to blame it on other people: the nurse in the hospital, my father (who, when he said Rich was a good choice, acted as if I had strolled into an appliance store and picked out the most energy-efficient refrigerator), and a friend of mine who once said, "It must be nice to fall in love when you're older. You're less neurotic about it. You have less expectations." I'd taken that comment badly, because I knew I'd once felt that neurotic about Hugo. I'd been willing to give everything up; I had been willing to be disinherited.

"Okay, Janie," my father once had shouted, "you want to go ahead and be with that Who-go, then go! Be with him! But don't expect any favors from me!"

"Who wants your favors?" I yelled.

"You want to pay your own way through school?"

"I hate school!"

"You want me to leave the house to your cousins?"

"Go ahead! I hate this house! I hate it!"

That was what I once had taken for love: heedlessness, carelessness, maudlin dramatics. I had long since grown past that. But even though I was mature enough to know that sort of emotion couldn't last, I still wanted to feel some intensity toward Rich. I didn't want a compromise. I couldn't bear to think we had married one another not as lovers but as pals, as two people who had sown their oats and were now ready to settle for second best, ready to sit back and let their children take a stab at finding passion. I'd pick a fight, I'd threaten to leave him, if only to disprove it.

Rich took a sip of his beer. His back was bothering him—he winced every time he shifted his legs from one step to another—and his glasses had slipped down on his nose, the way they always did when he was brooding. He put his beer down on the steps, then took my hand in his and turned the POW bracelet around my wrist to look at the inscription once again.

"It's weird you had the same bracelet Adrienne did," he said.

"What's weird about it? There were more people wearing bracelets than there were POWs. There had to be some overlap."

"But it's just such a strange coincidence that you both had William Redman."

"Well, we both had you, and you don't think that's strange," I said.

There was a snotty, defiant tone in my voice, and Rich picked up on it immediately. "What's the matter with you lately?" he asked.

"Nothing."

"You're always trying to pick a fight."

"I am not."

"There you go again. If you're mad about something, you should just talk about it."

"I'm upset about my father," I said.

"Okay," Rich said, warily. "I back off. Sorry."

He didn't believe me. That was okay. I didn't believe myself. I just wanted to get off the porch and get back inside. I wanted to retreat to my room and think about things.

"There's just so much stuff in the house," I said.

"It's pretty overwhelming. It's amazing what you collect over the years."

"We don't have that much," I said.

"We do if you really stop and think about it."

I couldn't seem to hold myself back. "It's not like we're going anywhere," I said. "It's not like we have to move it."

Rich looked down at his knuckles. I could tell he was considering letting that remark slip by, but then he thought better of it. "So you want to sell the house, then?"

"I don't know," I said. "I already told you. I don't like the idea of selling it, but there doesn't seem much reason to keep it."

Rich balled up his hand and rubbed at a spot of lint on his jeans. When he finally spoke, his voice came out too controlled, as if he had planned exactly what he was going to say. "Did you think any more about what we talked about the other day?"

"Yes."

"And?"

"I decided I wanted to do it."

"Well." He breathed a sigh. "That's really good news, Janie." He leaned over to hug me. I let him hold me against his shoulder, hoping that would melt that hard, nasty feeling I had inside. But it didn't work. I heard myself say, "But I don't want to have one right away."

"Next year, then?" Rich asked. When I didn't answer, he said, "It's not like we're getting any younger."

"I know."

"The longer we wait, the harder it's going to be."

"I know."

"All sorts of things could go wrong."

"I know it," I interrupted him. "And I said I'd think about it."

Rich sat there for a minute. "Thinking isn't good enough, Janie," he said. "You have to make up your mind."

He waited for me to answer. When it was obvious I had nothing to say, he stood up, then went back into the house, shutting the screen door behind him to keep it from slamming. Rich was always careful not to show any extreme emotion. That gave him an edge over me, who could keep nothing inside.

I sat on the porch for a while, trying not to let things get the best of me, but then my lips started to quiver and my face screwed up like a baby's when I thought about how complicated everything had gotten to be. I won't cry, I thought, I'll go inside and have another beer and forget about everything.

Inside, I could hear Rich thumping around in the crawl space upstairs. I went into the kitchen, where I didn't have to listen to him. The kitchen was a comforting room. The print on the wallpaper, of a man and woman riding along in a horse-drawn carriage, was faded, but still a sunny gold, and even though I thought it looked hideous, I liked the steady hum of the teapot-shaped clock. The counters were dusty and the sink streaked with white mineral deposits from the dripping faucet. It all looked so familiar and yet so foreign that I had to remind myself I once had lived here. I could live here again, I thought, if I wanted.

I took a beer out of the refrigerator, then tried to open the drawer that held the bottle opener. The drawer was stubborn. I had to yank on the handle before it slid forward suddenly, revealing a crazy jumble of things inside: twisties from plastic bags, red and white string from bakery boxes, corks crumbling at the edges, nail clippers, elastic bands, washers, corn skewers shaped like miniature cobs, and the single birthday candle my parents had put on my cake every year, that had once been marked, like a measuring stick, from one to eighteen.

Now it was just a stump of wax, burned down to the number seventeen. I reached out and touched it with one finger; then, on an impulse, I put it in my jeans pocket. I wanted to hang on to it. Rich and I had started a similar drawer in our kitchen, full of things we couldn't decide what to do with, things we couldn't bring ourselves to throw away, things our kids would have to clear out after we were gone. I felt sad when I realized how it hardly mattered where we lived, since clutter and chaos would always be tucked somewhere below the surface. But I found a little consolation in the thought that all over the world there existed millions of drawers just like this, one in every house.

Dutch Wife

Ever since he was a boy growing up in the suburbs of Miami, Tom Zogg had dreamed of the seasons. He longed to drag his feet through a pile of autumn leaves, trudge through a winter blizzard, splash in the downfall of a spring rain—and yet he had to live through day after day of summer, the endless repetition of the blazing sunrise, the bloated afternoon heat, the five o'clock torrential rain, and the sweltering multicolored sunset. The nights were hot. Oh, the lucky men who got to wear wool sweaters won Zogg's envy! Zogg lusted after long johns. He sighed deeply whenever he thought of argyle socks.

Since the day his father left his mother and disappeared somewhere in the general direction of north, "north" had sounded absolutely luscious on Zogg's tongue. He pictured Michigan as wild, woolly, and exotic; Indiana held more appeal to him than Madagascar or Mozambique. His fascination with cold climates dated back to a specific sweltering moment on Miami Beach. Zogg, six years old, was playing catch with a giant beach ball colored like a globe, the last gift his father had given him before he went away. Zogg stared at the ball, wondering why France was colored pink and China yellow. What made Australia light green? Why was Venezuela orange? Iceland, silver?

"Throw the ball!" Zogg's cousin screamed at him. But Zogg only clutched it tighter in his hands, putting a sizable dent in South America. "Throw the ball!" his malicious cousin repeated. When Zogg didn't respond, the cousin trotted over to the beach ball and punctured, with the safety pin that fastened his house keys to his bathing trunks, the drab gray speck of Poland. Zogg's world went phht in his hands. As he squinted in the glare of the sun, watching the globe slowly deflate, he craved to live in a colder, less impulsive climate.

That marked the beginning of Zogg's northern dreams. As a young boy, as a teenager, as a geography student at the University of Miami, Zogg walked the beach, the soles of his feet burning, imagining himself a hobo on a Canadian railroad line, an affable bum in Minneapolis. He was a pioneer striking out to settle unknown territory, a hunter with a coonskin cap jammed down on his frostbitten ears. He set iron-jawed traps for weasel and beaver. He bagged elk and pheasant and carried them home to the hearth, where he was greeted and embraced by the loving arms of his very own Pioneer Woman.

Whenever he thought of Pioneer Woman, hiding in that log cabin, miles away in the mysterious north, Zogg despaired. The great plains of the nation seemed to spread before him. He would have to travel miles to find her, shoot her down, and bag her. Zogg had never bagged any woman, be she pioneer or not. The very idea made him tremble. Big game hunting was not his specialty. Maps, land use, surveying— these were the sensible, concrete things he knew and loved.

He was trained to measure Florida, the marshes and the malls. But he was sick of the state. He couldn't reconcile the presence of alligators with the proliferation of the golden arches of McDonald's and the goofy facades of Chuck E Cheese. He longed for open spaces, the consistency of Antarctica.

One bright and sunny day as he was combing the want ads in *Surveyor's Guide* he heard the great hark and call of the northern wilds:

> Fire in county courthouse destroyed all maps. Seek responsible cartographer. Housing and vehicle provided for year-long position in Shy Beaver, South Dakota.

It was not as good as north, but it might do. Zogg sent in his application. An hour after he received his letter of acceptance, he was

down in the garment district, sweating as he purchased the very items
it made most Floridians hot just thinking about. *"Voy al norte,"* he
shyly confided to the Cuban shopkeeper.

"Crazy," the man said.

Maybe he was. He had plenty of time to think about it on the journey. Boarding a succession of ever-smaller planes, Zogg flew from
Miami to Chicago to Minneapolis to Sioux Falls to Shy Beaver. His
ears clogged and his head ached from the roar of the last, tiniest Piper,
on which he was the sole passenger. He leaned his head against the
window, staring miles below at the patchwork fields of corn, soy, and
alfalfa laid out like a warm quilt over a large, soft bed. The plane
landed with a bump. Zogg gathered up his windbreaker and exited.

The sky hung farther above him than ever before in his life. Zogg
marveled at it.

"Bird-watching?" a voice said.

Zogg quickly lowered his head and found himself staring at the
metal buttons of a red flannel shirt. He looked up again, into the blue
eyes of a balding blond giant.

"Bert Dusseldorf," the giant said. "Sheriff of Shy Beaver."

Zogg extended his hand and let Dusseldorf's paw agitate his whole
body up and down.

"Thomas Zogg—what kind of name is that? Hungarian? Polish?"

"I'm a mixture."

"We were hoping for a Methodist. Oh well. No matter." Dusseldorf
reached down and clasped Zogg's two oversized suitcases, abandoned
next to the plane. "Follow me."

Dazed by the great expanse of sky above his head and the wind
sweeping in off the fields, Zogg lagged behind.

Dusseldorf turned. "Drop something?"

Zogg shook his head and half galloped over to where Dusseldorf
was slinging his suitcases, like the carcasses of slaughtered animals,
into the bed of a blue pickup truck.

"Heavy trunks," Dusseldorf said. "You got your girlfriend in there?"

"No sir."

"So you left her back home. Well, there's plenty of blond ones right here. They don't call this virgin territory for nothing!" Dusseldorf waited for Zogg to acknowledge his joke before he indulged in his own reaction. "Uh huh!" he said, giving Zogg a hearty slap on the back that catapulted him into the open door of the truck and sent him sprawling on the front seat. Momentarily stunned and winded, Zogg brushed the dust off his stiff new jeans and squinted at a sticker attached to the black dashboard. It pictured two lascivious-looking swine saluting each other with champagne glasses. Bubbles rose in the air. BACON IN THE MAKIN'! the sticker read.

Zogg sighed with satisfaction. He was home.

The pollen-laden September air made Zogg sneeze. Fields of corn whizzed by as Dusseldorf drove on, the rear tires of the truck leaving a hurricane cloud of dust in its wake. Zogg had been on many a roller coaster, but he enjoyed far more this swift passage into the unknown. He almost resented it when Dusseldorf broke the mystery.

"We're putting you up at Aunt Adeline's."

Somehow Zogg hadn't reckoned with Aunt Adeline.

"She died last winter, when the snow was five feet on the ground. Lies six foot under on the hill behind the church," said Dusseldorf. "Helluva time digging her grave."

Zogg nodded respectfully.

"And a helluva time carrying that coffin up the hill," Dusseldorf said. "By God, she was a fat one. But Adeline Dusseldorf always was trouble. Why, she never got married," he exclaimed, as if that explained it all. "Died an unplowed field. That's rare in these parts."

Dusseldorf looked at Zogg, who, for want of any better response, cracked a nervous smile.

"Haw!" Dusseldorf said. He leaned the flat of his hand on the horn. The horn took a moment to warm up before it echoed back Dusseldorf's own sense of jubilation.

"Look sharp," he said. "Here's the Beaver."

As they pulled into the town square, all sorts of fertile, sexy jazz filled Zogg's head. Behind the brick facade of the one drugstore, one bank, one bar, one post office, he imagined Pioneer Woman was waiting. Perhaps she was selecting a spool of thread in the general store, or watching while the proprietor fetched a can of early spring peas from the highest shelf. She fingered the bolts of fabric stacked upon a table. "I'll have four yards of this red plaid," she said, adding with a bride's shy smile, "I'm sewing Tom a shirt for his birthday." Yes, that was it. She would sew for him, cook for him, completely un-Zogg him. She would transform him from a skinny little surveyor into a virile, rugged Pioneer Man.

In front of the town hall the pickup hit a bump. Zogg sneezed, shook himself out of his reverie, and stared at the tall, broad-shouldered women crossing the square, the tall, broader-shouldered farmers, veritable Norse gods in faded overalls and seed-feed caps. His stomach felt hollow. He cleared his throat. "I notice the people up here are a bit on the big side."

"Regular tractor trailers, the whole lot of us. You'll stick out like a sore—uh huh!—Tom Thumb, you get it?"

"Got it."

Dusseldorf leaned over and slapped him on the thigh. Zogg felt as though his kneecap was about to shatter. Dusseldorf leaned on the horn and the horn hiccuped back. He stepped on the gas pedal and the truck shot out of town and onto another dirt road.

"Now that girl of yours back home, Thomas—"

"What girl?"

"She a college girl?"

"There really wasn't any—"

"Now, Thomas, we don't play coy up here. Why else would you leave Miami if it weren't for a little girl trouble?"

"Sheriff Dusseldorf—"

"Call me Bert, Bert, by golly. And cheer up. We've got lots of fine, solid girls up here, Thomas. I lay mind one of 'em will want to see what Florida has to offer."

Zogg sneezed, then braced himself for another whack on the knee or a punch on the arm. But Dusseldorf merely leaned on the horn again.

"We're coming onto the back of my farm."

"I thought you were sheriff."

"Sheriff doesn't amount to much. Investigate a couple of cases of cabin fever in February. Ride over to the reservation and say 'how' every now and then to the Injuns. They have Injuns where you live?"

"No. But there are Cubans."

"What are they like?"

"Small, with dark hair."

"Just like you," Dusseldorf said. "You're the same size as Didi. My daughter. Exactly your height. Bakes a mean pork chop. That's important, since her mother died."

Zogg nodded respectfully. At the thought of pork chops, his empty, airsick stomach grumbled. He wondered if Didi would have dinner waiting. The wooden picnic table he spotted as they drove up to Dusseldorf's dirty white farm house fired his imagination. He conjured up the smell of cole slaw, potato salad, baked beans. "Is the meal to your liking?" the domesticated Didi of Zogg's dreams asked him as she sashayed, in a ruffled peasant dress, around the table. "You care for chocolate cake or apple pie for dessert?"

The pickup jerked to a stop in front of the house. The wide front porch was empty. The porch swing tipped lazily in the wind, but the wind carried no smell of chops, no sweet fragrance of pie. It carried the smell of manure and the itch of pollen. Zogg wiped his nose on his last remaining Kleenex. When he got out of the cab, the ground moved dizzily beneath his feet. He cocked an ear. Garbled music blossomed forth from the open doors of the sprawling, ramshackle red barn.

"That's Didi." Dusseldorf climbed out of the truck. "And her trombone. By golly, that noise drives me batty. In the summer I make her play in the barn. Chases the rats away."

A spitty, gargly rendition of "For He's a Jolly Good Fellow" echoed out of the doorway, every fourth or fifth note off.

"By God, that sounds god-awful," Dusseldorf said. Softly, he sang the last phrase of the song, emphasizing each note that Didi mangled. "Which—nobody—can—deny. Goddamn! She always goes up on that last note. It's supposed to go down, go down, which nobody can de-nyyyy. DIDI!"

"What?" a high-pitched holler returned.

"It's supposed to go down!"

"The music says go up!"

Dusseldorf shook his head. "She's about as musical as a hill of beans," he told Zogg. Raising his voice, he called, "Mr. Zogg is here. Come on out and say howdy."

From the dark interior of the barn emerged a thin, adolescent figure with lank blond hair, all gangly arms and knock-kneed legs. Three scraggly barn cats purred and nuzzled around her emaciated ankles and dirty white sneakers. The orange shorts outfit Didi wore accentuated the bones at the base of her neck and threw into relief her spindly elbows and the inward curve of her painfully skinny knees. Didi's knees were the ugliest Zogg had ever seen in his life. They came together as if to embrace and kiss, and as if the kiss had been violent, the right knee sported a large bruise that flowered in blue, green, purple, and mustard-colored splendor. Zogg saw the bruise as a map of the world, containing the colors of mountains, rivers, and oceans.

He scoured its depths and climbed its heights. He paddled across its waters. The sheer expanse was difficult to fathom . . . its immensity was blinding . . .

Zogg blinked. "Where'd you get that black and blue?"

"Tripped on a mousetrap," Didi said. "You like a pop?"

"A what?"

"A pop. A soder pop."

"A cool drink sounds good," Dusseldorf said. "Get us both one, Didi."

Didi raised her horn to her mouth, puffed out her cheeks, and answered with a protesting toot. Dusseldorf shook his head as he watched her rattle her bones up the rickety front porch.

"Soon as she turned thirteen, she turned loony tunes," he said.

Zogg watched the brass of her trombone glint, once, in the sun.

Didi's pork chops were indeed the meanest Zogg had ever wrestled with in his life. They were crisp with burnt thyme and dry on the inside. His ears, clogged from the many ups and downs of the plane flights, crackled with each chomp of the jaw. His relationship with Didi's fresh garden salad fared no better. The carrots grated on his teeth and the distinct flavor of dirt dressed the lettuce. Zogg was miserably hungry. His root beer soda pop, fizzing with cracked ice, was his sole relief.

While Dusseldorf and Didi silently chowed down their dinner, Zogg contented himself with reading the embroidered samplers that hung on the wall in every available space that wasn't covered by a tarnished copper pot hanging from a nail. *Home is where the heart is,* a fancy cross-stitch proclaimed. *It takes a heap a' lovin' to make a house a home.* On the counter, a cookie jar in the shape of a pig said, *Go on, make a hog of yourself!*

"You're looking hungry, Thomas," Dusseldorf said. With his fork, he stabbed another flat slab of pork off the serving platter and dropped it, with a clang, on Zogg's plate. "We'll need to fatten you up by winter. By God, I've never seen a man so malnourished in my life. What do they feed you in Florida?"

"Crocodiles," Didi said. "And snakes."

"Crocodiles are African," Zogg said. "And I don't think downtown Miami has seen a snake for—"

"Gila monsters," Didi continued, "and pink flamingos and monkeys. I've been reading a book all about it."

"Don't pay attention to her, Thomas," Dusseldorf said. "Just keep on eating."

"Did you notice how skinny I was?" Didi asked Zogg. She held her transparent wrist across the table for his inspection. Her blue eyes shone with excitement. "I eat like a hog, but I'm the only Dusseldorf since they came over in a covered wagon that isn't fat. My grandfather was fat and my grandmother was fat and my dad is fat—"

"I am not fat," Dusseldorf said.

"He broke a pew in church once, Mr. Zogg—"

"Tell it right. It was Addie's weight that did that pew in."

"And my Great-Aunt Adeline was the fattest woman you ever seen in your life. She should have joined a circus. 'Why, what in the world would I do in a circus, Didi?' she used to ask, and I used to say, 'Just stand up there on a platform and folks will pay to see it jiggle.' But she didn't want to join even if she could get rich, because she didn't want to live in a mini-home trailer on wheels with dwarfs and pickled babies and such. 'I'd sooner die,' she said, 'than not have a flower garden.' Turned out she died even though she didn't join the circus. You coming to church with us tomorrow?"

Before Zogg could answer, Dusseldorf said, "Thomas is not of our persuasion."

"Are you persuaded Catholic?"

Zogg shook his head.

"Good thing," Didi said. "They're cannibals." She opened her mouth wide and shoveled in a forkful of pork chop.

"We hope you'll be happy here," Dusseldorf told Zogg. "Aunt Adeline's house is nice and warm, and there's a flower garden that'll overwhelm you come spring."

"And there's two bathrooms and a Wurlitzer pianna," Didi said. "And nobody to talk to for miles around, except me."

"You're welcome anytime for dinner," Dusseldorf said. "If you like Didi's pork chops, wait until you try her fried chicken."

"Tongue's my real specialty," Didi said, and stuck her own out at Zogg. It was long, pink, and beaded with saliva. "You want to spend the night?"

"Beg pardon?"

"We need to fix things up a bit at Addie's," Dusseldorf said.

"You can sleep in my room," Didi said, "but you have to promise not to read my diary."

"Thomas doesn't care about your diary, Didi."

"You don't?"

The vistas of adolescence, suddenly open to Zogg, seemed appealing. "I can't say I wouldn't be tempted," he told Didi.

That satisfied her. "You'd be too scared to read it. On the first page I drew a skull and crossbones and a sign that says ANCIENT VOODOO CURSE: KEEP YOUR FAT HANDS OFF!"

Zogg felt his head starting to ache.

"Didi," Dusseldorf said firmly, "go change your sheets."

Didi rose from the table, reached under her orange shorts in the back, and pulled her underwear down with a snap. She galloped off, sneakers like thunder on the bare wooden stairs.

Dusseldorf shook his head. "She ain't a boy and she ain't a girl. By God if she doesn't belong in a circus herself." He took a swig of his root beer. "Well, make yourself at home, Thomas. In the parlor we got a color TV and plenty of copies of the *Digest*."

Zogg sat on the porch swing after supper, the steady creak of the chains drowning out the protests of his stomach. The sun was setting, but the heavy golden orb he was accustomed to seeing sink over the beach was nothing more than a slightly orange haze settling over the fields. There was nothing dramatic about it. It simply passed away, the way an old man might stop breathing. Then, suddenly, it was dark. No crickets sang, no birds screeched. Zogg sat alone, abandoned, in a big black sea of corn and soybeans.

The porch light snapped on.

"He's just sitting there," Zogg heard Didi report to Dusseldorf. "And guess what? He's so short his feet don't touch the porch when he's on the swing."

"Tell him to come on in, before he gets bitten alive by mosquitoes."

Didi stepped onto the porch, letting the screen door slam. "My dad says to come on in before you get bitten alive by vampire bats. They live under the eaves, and if you've ever seen *Dracula*, you know those things are mighty vicious."

Zogg followed Didi back into the house. In the rocking chair by the fireplace he settled down and read an issue of *Reader's Digest* from front to back. At his rolltop desk, Dusseldorf sighed over his accounts; lying on her stomach on the braided rug, Didi read the comics. Zogg tried not to look at the white rim of underwear peeking out from under her shorts. Every now and then her spine knotted up as she chuckled. "Charlie Brown's a good one tonight," she reported. "Gasoline Alley is okay, too."

"Dick Tracy's in hot water," Dusseldorf said. The bald spot on the back of his head shone under his desk lamp. "Pogo is philosophizing as usual."

"You think Juliet Jones will ever have a baby?"

"She'd best get married first, or the *Beaver Times* won't carry that strip long enough for us to see the announcement."

"They announce plenty of other shotgun weddings."

"So sayeth who?"

"Aunt Adeline."

"By God, if I knew she was talking to you about things like that—"

"You said it was natural for farm kids to talk about the birds and the bees—"

"Not in front of Thomas, Didi."

"Why? Doesn't he know about them?"

Zogg raised his *Reader's Digest* and hid behind "Life in These United States." He felt his face flush red. He was glad when Didi finally got up to close the front door. "That's to keep the killer bats out," she explained. "Sometimes they eat their way right through the screen when they smell the pork chops in your blood."

Dusseldorf gave out a gargantuan yawn. "You're welcome to stay up and watch TV with Didi."

Zogg tentatively tried out his new northern vocabulary. "Nope, it's time for me to hit the hay."

"Where'd you hear that gooped-up expression?" Didi asked. "On a western?" She smiled fiendishly. "Yippy-i-oh-ky-yea!"

Didi's room was papered in pink stripes, the high four-poster bed covered with a pink and white quilt, and the window dressed in fussy ruffles. On the white chest of drawers stood a framed photograph of a younger Dusseldorf and a big-chested blond woman—Didi's mother, no doubt. Books on dinosaurs and an entire set of Hardy Boys mysteries lined the white bookshelves. In the corner stood a piece of furniture Zogg thought girls called a vanity. He wondered what Didi was doing with a perfume table. Curiosity seized him. He closed the bedroom door and carefully, quietly raised the vanity's lid. With a loud squeak a soft, pliable object jumped out at him like a jack-in-the-box. Zogg slammed the lid down in fright. His heart beat quickly. Discovered! Caught red-handed, in the act! He creaked on the wooden floorboards over to where the jumping object lay on the pink rug. It was an ugly green toy snake, about a yard long; its coils could be suppressed to make it pop forward if pressure suddenly was released on the top. With a gold pin a small note was attached to the bottom of the snake, sloppily scribbled on pink writing paper. KEEP YOUR FAT HANDS OFF MY DIARY AND THIS MEANS YOU!

Zogg fingered the gold safety pin, suddenly reminded of its double that, sixteen years ago, had punctured his precious ball on Miami Beach. Maybe he was more at home than he thought. Embarrassed and penitent, he pressed down the coils of the snake and tried to quietly replace it inside the vanity. Didi's pink diary lay in the back corner. Zogg noticed a flash of gold on the side and remembered that at the dinner table she had fiddled with a chain around her neck, a chain he had assumed held a charm or a cross. Now he was fairly certain it held the key to the diary's gold lock. Even if he had wanted to read her innermost thoughts, he wouldn't have been able to get at them anyway.

Exhausted, he turned off the light, stripped to his shorts, turned back the quilt, and fell face forward onto the sheets. This was sleep, Miami-style, the cool air denied to him during the day welcome to flow over his body in the evening. He slept soundly. Come morning, the bedroom door clicked. Zogg's eyes flickered open to a room of blazing pink sunlight. He immediately shut his eyes. Didi—who else?—tiptoed in. Zogg shivered in his nakedness. What was she doing? No drawers rattled open. No closet doors squeaked. Zogg was infinitely glad he lay on his stomach. He prayed his underwear was reasonably clean, all the while knowing it was not.

Didi was inspecting him. Zogg's nose tickled. He raised his head and sneezed.

"I was just picking out my church dress!" Didi turned her back, opened the closet, and pushed hanger after hanger from one side of the rod to the other.

"You're taking your sweet time."

"I've got a lot of dresses."

Zogg reached down and yanked up the quilt. "Anybody ever tell you that staring at somebody in bed is like reading somebody's diary?"

Didi yanked out an ugly orange ruffled dress. "Anybody ever tell you that you got skin as dark as an Injun?" She stomped over to her vanity, pulled out the snake, and popped it in Zogg's general direction, missing by a long shot. The door slammed behind her.

"It's a tan!" he called out after her. To console himself, he muttered, "Something you damn Injun-haters know nothing whatsoever about."

He dropped his head back onto the pillow and continued to sleep. When he awoke the pink of the wallpaper was less bright, less vibrant. His watch said 11:30.

What Dusseldorf referred to as "the washroom" was at the end of the hall. Zogg pulled on his jeans, half buttoned his shirt, and headed out. The Dusseldorfs had an old-fashioned claw-foot tub and a wooden medicine cabinet. Zogg used a white face cloth imprinted with the words "Minneapolis Motor Lodge" and a bath towel that boasted the name of the Cheyenne Budget Inn. So Dusseldorf was a law-enforcing thief. Or maybe it was Didi who had stuffed the motel towels into an ancient, heavy suitcase that snapped shut with noisy gold clasps, borrowed from her namesake, Aunt Adeline.

Zogg took a leisurely bath, in which he pretended he was Columbus on the high seas. His men were discontent. They were starving to death, wasting away with scurvy and rickets. Mutiny threatened the voyage of the Nina, the Pinta, and the Santa Maria. But lo! What sight broke upon the cold, vast horizon? "Land!" shouted the little monkey of a man who had climbed to the top of the mainsail. Columbus was back in business. "Hoist those sails!" he commanded. "Steer her fast. All men on the poop deck—"

Someone was banging on the door. In the rapidly cooling bath water, Zogg stopped splashing and sat perfectly still.

"My dad wants to know what you want for breakfast even though it's already time for lunch."

Zogg stared at the carved brass doorknob, half expecting to see it turn and Didi enter. He was sure her eye was at the keyhole. "What are my options?" he called back.

"You can have oatmeal or grits or shredded wheat with raisins on top," Didi called out in a bored voice. "You can have eggs and hash browns and bacon and sausage and ham. You can have blueberry pancakes or strawberry pancakes, only the strawberries are frozen, not fresh from the garden, or you can have plain old pancakes or French toast and waffles—"

"What did you have?"

"Cheerios and a glass of milk."

Columbus rose from his bath water and wrapped Cheyenne around his skinny little fanny. "I'll be right down," he said.

After Zogg's breakfast—and Didi and the sheriff's lunch—Dusseldorf hoisted Zogg's suitcases back into the pickup and drove over to Aunt Adeline's. Didi was left behind to show Zogg the best way to walk. She still had on her orange church dress. The hem hit above her knee, and the bruise that had so fascinated Zogg the day before now seemed duller. Didi took off her white patent leather shoes and slipped on her dirty sneakers without any socks. "You want to go the easy way or the hard way?"

"What does the hard way involve?"

"Cutting through the corn. But you can't get lost, 'cause if you do you're liable to freeze overnight and die, and then when harvest comes the combine'll cut you down like just another stalk, mash you up, thresh you out, and you'll be just another corn muffin, a-sitting on our breakfast table."

"We'll take the corn, then."

"Last one through is a rotten egg!" Didi flew down the front steps and disappeared, a streak of orange, into the more than head-high acre. Zogg quickly followed, arms thrashing left and right to keep the dried, scratchy stalks off his face. It didn't work. The stiff leaves cut the palms of his hands and wrists; a huge ear of corn, as giant a variety of the species that he had ever seen, brained him. His ears rang. He stopped to sneeze. When he looked up, Didi was long gone. The stalks that she had pushed aside had bounced back into place. There was only Zogg, the great blue sky, and corn. Zogg breathed heavily with fear.

"Whooo-ooo," Didi called, like an owl, from ahead. Zogg forged forward like an explorer. The field felt as long as forever. When Zogg finally surfaced into the open, Didi greeted him, her right hand pinching her snub nose.

"Pee-u, I smell a rotten egg."

Zogg sneezed. "You little bitch!"

Didi unplugged her nose. Her lower lip hung down. "I'm gonna tell my dad you said that."

"And I'll tell your dad you were in my room this morning staring at me—"

"That's my room! And I think I'll tell him you were trying to read my diary."

"I'll tell him you set me a trap. I'll tell him you were peeking through the keyhole while I was in the bathtub—"

"The keyhole!" Didi snorted. "You were the one who left the door an inch open."

"And you were the one who stole those towels from the Minneapolis Motor Lodge."

"I did not!" Didi stomped her sneaker on the hard ground. "My mom did, on her honeymoon. I wasn't even born yet."

Zogg fell silent at the mention of Didi's dead mother. "All right. I'm sorry." A big, wet, sloppy tear rolled down the left side of Didi's face. "Hey, look, I don't have a father, and you don't see me blubbering like a baby."

With the palm of her hand, Didi smeared the tear away. "I hate you. No wonder your girlfriend jilted you in Florida. I know, 'cause I heard my dad telling everyone after church today."

"Let's get this straight," Zogg said. "I don't have a girlfriend."

"Not anymore, you don't."

Zogg sneezed in protest. Didi offered the white sash of her dress for him to blow his nose on. "If I was a medicine man," she said, "I'd say you had a devil trapped inside your head. Then I'd do a dance to make it go away."

That sweet apology softened Zogg. He politely refused Didi's sash, and used the forearm of his shirt to wipe his nose.

"Here's Aunt Adeline's." Didi pointed to the white gables that stood like cathedral spires in the blue sky. The farmhouse had a porch that ran around two sides, maybe three—Zogg couldn't tell from where he was standing. Dusseldorf stood on the steps. He came forward to meet them.

"What the hell," he said, as Zogg drew closer. "You cut yourself shaving?"

Zogg lifted his hands to his face. Tiny dots of blood came away.

"We cut through the corn," Didi said.

Dusseldorf shook his head. "If I knew you better, Thomas, I'd say you were a dang fool."

"Go ahead. My mother says it all the time."

"He doesn't have a father," Didi reported. "Too bad you didn't know this morning, or you could have told everybody about that after church, too." She jumped up and down on the ground in front of the porch. "Look, this here's the storm cellar. You hide here when a twister hits." She leaned down to grasp the handle of a heavy wooden door implanted in the grass like a horizontal tombstone. She heaved the door open, revealing a square of hollowed-out earth about seven feet deep and five feet across. In one dark corner of the square, a long pinkish-brown earthworm writhed.

"You want to hear a good one about this cellar?" Didi asked, and plowed on before Dusseldorf could stop her. "Once at the end of winter, Aunt Addie pulled it open and found the body of a dead Injun. He was frozen like a slab of meat, with a five-inch survival knife stuck straight through his heart and a whiskey bottle in his hand."

Zogg's blood pulsed the way it used to when, as a boy, sitting in front of the black and white TV, he watched the climactic scene of a western.

"Tell it right, Didi," Dusseldorf said. "Don't exaggerate."

"So Aunt Adeline was so scared she had a brain seizure. She had a heart attack and fainted and fell right into here, slam-bang on top of that frozen Injun. I already told you she was a fat one. When she came to, she found she couldn't get out of here if her life depended on it. She was hollering and hollering for half an hour before me and my dad heard her and came to help her out. 'Murder, murder!' she kept hollering."

"She never hollered, 'Murder,' " Dusseldorf said.

"Oh, that's right. She hollered, 'Rape!' So we came running over and my dad had his gun and he found her and said, 'Addie, you kill that Injun?' and she said, 'I swear on the holiest Bible I have never seen the likes of this damn man in my life.' My dad sure was relieved Aunt Addie hadn't knifed him. 'You never know with Addie,' he said."

"Didi, shut your trap," Dusseldorf said.

Didi only opened it wider. "TIMBER!" she yelled, and tipped the storm cellar door back to the earth with a thud that resounded throughout the countryside.

"How much do you think that door weighs?" Zogg asked.

"Oh, a couple of hundred pounds easily," Didi said.

As he followed Dusseldorf and Didi up the wooden porch steps, Zogg used his left hand to feel his upper right arm. He'd never build up enough muscle to heave open that door. If a twister came, he'd be like Dorothy in Kansas, pulling futilely at the handle while a gray funnel cloud cut a path through the corn, whirling closer and closer until it finally gathered him up and carried him, not to Oz, but up into the sky and on to heaven, where he would be greeted by the fat Aunt Adeline. She held a plate of baked chicken in her hands. "You care for wings?" she asked. "Or can I interest you in a breast?"

"There's a deadbolt on this door," Dusseldorf explained as he took the keys out of his pocket.

"You've got to be careful you don't shut yourself out," Didi said, "or you'll freeze yourself solid dead, just like that Injun."

Dusseldorf cursed as he fiddled with the door. "Goddang key. Goddang Adeline. The only house in the entire Beaver with a lock on it."

"I guess she was afraid of Injuns," Zogg offered.

"Nope. Rapists!" Didi said, as her father popped open the lock. "Too fat to fight back. Make sure you leave your shoes in the front hall in the winter. Aunt Adeline was particular about her carpet."

Zogg followed Didi into the parlor. It was like entering a budding flower garden. The wallpaper was studded with tiny pink peonies, and the large overstuffed armchairs bloomed in red, white, and pink slipcovers. The carpet Aunt Adeline was so fussy about was a hothouse of roses, and the curtains, although white, budded in ruffle after ruffle. Several huge green vases of carnations proliferated on the mantel.

"Aunt Addie was fond of her flowers," Dusseldorf said.

"So I noticed," Zogg said. He sank down on the sofa-rosebed. The cushion creaked, and a loose spring jabbed him in the rump like a prickly thorn.

Dusseldorf went into the basement to check the furnace and hot water heater. Didi perched opposite Zogg on a needlepoint cushion of lilies. Her bruised knee curved inward like a bow. "This whole house is mine," she said. "I inherited it from Aunt Adeline."

"So you'll live here when you grow up."

"Oh, I don't know," Didi said vaguely, mysteriously. "Depends on what I become."

"What do you want to be?"

"A marine biologist."

Zogg bit his lip to keep from laughing. "You'd be hard pressed to find a river around here, never mind an ocean."

"Well, maybe I'll just be Tarzan the Apeman, then. Or maybe I'll move here and play the trombone and get fat until I die." She wound a strand of blond hair around her little finger. A stream of light hit her face from the window and she squinted. "What'd you come here for, anyway? Why'd you really, really come here?"

Gazing around Aunt Adeline's fabric greenhouse and feeling the onslaught of another sneeze, Zogg began to wonder. "I guess I've always wanted to see snow."

"So why don't you just look at pictures? My dad says pictures are better than the real thing because they leave out all the bad parts. I've always wanted to see the ocean, but my dad, he says, 'Didi, figure a fold-out accordion of postcards will show you the ocean quite nicely.' " She scratched her ear. "I think that's stupid. I want to see the real thing. What's the real ocean like?"

Zogg thought about it for a moment. It was green. It was big. When the weather was mild and the tide went out, you felt as though you could walk on the sandbar to the ends of the earth. When there was a storm, the waves kicked up mounds of seaweed, and after a hurricane, piles of dead, slimy fish littered the beach. The sand was hot, and you had to be careful not to scald your feet. The air smelled of cocoa butter and tar and oil from the huge ships that maneuvered in and out of the harbor. Radios softly played. Zogg felt flooded with warmth.

"Well?" Didi demanded. "What's it like?"

"It's just beautiful, that's all. It's the most magnificent thing on earth. You could just sit in front of it and dream all day." His throat hurt when he remembered he wouldn't see it, now, for an entire year. "What's snow like?" he asked.

She scrunched up her face. "It's white and it comes down in piles and piles and it makes everything look the same and boring. It's cold

and it's quiet, so quiet I have to play my trombone just to blast it all
away—"

A loud crack snapped inside the piano, and a discord of notes
sounded. Zogg looked over just in time to see two keys in the middle
of the keyboard depress and slowly rise back up. Didi jumped up from
her lily patch. "Caught one!"

"A ghost?"

"Do you like mice?" Didi asked. " 'Cause there's a whole lot of
'em living here, especially inside the pianna. So far I've caught twelve
in the traps." She tiptoed over to the piano and smiled maliciously as
she opened the lid and peered within. "Yup, here's number thirteen,
a baker's dozen. Gotcha, little sucker!"

Zogg's stomach, still a little airsick, turned a full revolution. He
closed his eyes as Didi calmly chattered away. "First time we knew
we had a problem was after Aunt Addie died and my dad reached into
the cupboard for a cookie and found all these little turds lying around.
He almost put one in his mouth 'cause he thought it was a raisin. Then
he says, 'Looks like you got a mouse in your house, Didi,' and then lo
and behold, we discovered a mouse had drilled a tunnel right through
a package of Fig Newtons. So I kept a couple of the barn cats over
here to eat 'em up, but then I'd come over and find little mousie parts
all over the place, so I chucked the cats out and set traps. Now I come
over and clean 'em out every day, 'cause if I don't the other mice get
hungry and eat the guts out of the mouse that's been trapped, just the
way hogs will eat another hog that's keeled over from the heat in the
pen—"

"Oh, stop!" Zogg put his hands to his ears and opened his eyes.
Before him stood Didi, one skinny, scrawny creature holding another
skinny, scrawny gray creature by the tail.

"You aren't scared of 'em, are you?"

Zogg shuddered. "I'm more used to cockroaches."

"Oh, insects," Didi said. "That's nothing."

"Cockroaches in Florida are as big as the palm of your hand," Zogg said. "Some fly."

"Like bats?" Didi shrieked and dropped the mouse. "Why'd you tell me that? I hate bats!"

"Mice and bats are second cousins."

Didi shrieked again.

Dusseldorf lumbered around the corner. "Furnace is okay. Hot water heater is—goddangit, Didi, what are you hollering about now?"

"Bats!"

"Now we got bats too?" Dusseldorf asked. He spotted the mouse on the carpet. "Throw that rodent away."

Didi picked up the mouse and marched out the front door. Through the window, Zogg watched her toss it, like a Frisbee, over the porch rail toward the cornfield. She slammed the front door when she came back in, dusting her hands on her orange church dress.

"Soap and water," Dusseldorf said. "Soap and water!"

Didi stomped into the kitchen. Zogg, embarrassed to be caught in the middle of yet another domestic quarrel, turned to some photographs on the table next to him. His eye was drawn to a silver frame, filigreed with flowers, surrounding the picture of a thin, blond girl in a flour-sack dress—high collar, ruffled sleeves, hem to the ground, dropped waist. She stood in a garden, snapdragons lapping about her ankles, eyes narrowed into a squint.

"Didi looks older in this picture," Zogg said.

"Ain't Didi. It's Addie, in her younger days."

"I thought you said Addie was fat."

"She used to be skinny," Didi announced, coming back in. "But then her boyfriend jilted her, and she ate and ate just to spite her own face. By the way—" She turned to her father. "He hasn't been jilted."

"Now, Thomas," Dusseldorf said, "you can tell us the truth. We know the only sane reason a man would leave sunny Florida to come to this godforsaken place is because his girl threw him over."

"He says he came to see snow," Didi said.

Dusseldorf looked at Zogg to confirm it. Zogg nodded. "Well," Dusseldorf said. "Boy. You're going to see a helluva lot of it." He scratched his ear. "Maybe you better let on you've been jilted anyhow. You tell folks you came here to see snow, they're liable to think you're tetched."

Zogg was not tetched. But staring at the photograph—Pioneer Woman trapped within the silver picture frame—he was positive he'd been born into the wrong century.

"He's already invited us back to Florida," Didi said. "He said he'd take me to Disneyworld and I'm going to see the ocean."

"I just got here." Zogg dug his heels into the carpet to defend his squatting rights.

"You can't stay in Shy Beaver forever," Didi said. "Nobody would marry you. You're too short, and even though you're nice, you're still a furriner from the outside world."

"Yup," Dusseldorf said, "Addie was the last one here to get caught up with that kind."

"And look what happened to her!" Didi exclaimed, her eyes shining.

"What did happen?" Zogg asked.

"I'm not telling you until you take me to Disneyworld."

"All hell will freeze over before any man takes you anywhere," Dusseldorf said. He looked at Zogg. "Isn't that right?"

The rest of Aunt Adeline's house was as chintzed-up as the front parlor. Flowers were everywhere—stenciled on the cabinets and baseboards, captured in color photographs and delicate watercolor pictures, pressed behind glass frames and dried into crumbly petals in jars in the bathroom. Zogg spent a good fifteen minutes searching through the linen cabinet for a plain white pillowcase before he gave up and resigned himself to spending the night with his face lying in a bed of purple petunias.

A mouse, long, gray, and thin, scooted across the floor in the bedroom. Zogg yelped, pounced onto Aunt Adeline's bed, and hid his head under the covers. His sleep was restless and his dreams marked by images from the John Deere farm machinery calendar he had seen hanging inside the linen closet. The calendar was dated 1969. The first man had landed on the moon, and Didi Dusseldorf hadn't even been born yet. A world without Didi. Already, Zogg had trouble imagining it.

The next day, after spending hours down at the county seat with Dusseldorf, inspecting the scene of the fire and dusting off some ancient surveying equipment, Zogg once again sat down to Didi's pork chops. When Didi begged her father to help her with her first seventh-grade English assignment—an autobiography—Zogg gallantly stepped in and volunteered. Didi smiled wickedly. "I knew you'd help out," she said, handing him the essay.

THE LIFE STORIE OF ADELINE HILDA DUSSELDORF THE SECOND
BY ADELINE HILDA DUSSELDORF THE SECOND

My name is Adeline Hilda Dusseldorf but my dad he calls me Didi because I used to have an aunt named Addie. I am thirtene years old and have traveled to all the principle cities of South Dakota and visited Black Hills and Custer's Battlefield and I saw Mount Rushmore once but there was too much fog. The furthest I have ever been from Shy Beaver is Sioux City where we took a tour of the stockyard in sixth grade.

I live with my dad and he tells jokes that nobody laughs at but him. My mother is dead.

DUTCH WIFE

I am thirtene years old and I play the trumbone but I really would rather be a baton twirler or a drum majurette.

I have eight uncles and eight aunts and exactly twenty-six cousins. My principle claim to fame besides being so skinny is that I have five uncles on my dad's side named Bert: Albert, Elbert, Hilbert, Wilbert, and Diebert. My dad's name is just plain old Bert because by the time he was born my grandad had run out of other kinds of Bert and he figured one of them at least ought to sound American.

My best friend is Mr. Thomas Zogg. He's from Flurida and has visited all the principle cities of Flurida like Miami. He has been to Cuba and has shaken Fido Castro's hand, which means he's a comunist. He has wrestled crocodiles and eaten pink flamingos for supper. He really likes my pork chops best, though. He has swum in the great Atlantic Ocean. He knows how to speak Spanish and he's afraid of mice but that's ok since I hate bats. He has a college education.

Mr. Thomas Zogg is not of our persuasion which means he isn't Methodist. He is here to see the snow and to pick out a new girlfriend. Mr. Thomas Zogg is exactly my hite and size but next year my dad says I'll probably be bigger than he ever will be because he is already a fully grown man even though he looks only half grown. When she was seventeen my Aunt Adeline fell in love with a short man from Canada and it was all downhill from there.

The End

"Now look here, Didi," Zogg said, "I have never wrestled a crocodile in my life. It's *Fidel,* not *Fido* Castro, and where'd you get the crazy idea I'm a Communist?"

"My dad's got a bet going with one of my Uncle Berts—"

Zogg snatched the pen out of Didi's hand. "Why don't you learn how to spell, you little idiot?" Furiously, he corrected all the *principles* to *principals,* and inserted an *o* in every *Flurida.* "Some autobiography. It's more about me than you."

Didi pouted. "You've been to Disneyworld," she said. "You're more interesting."

After a month in Aunt Adeline's bed, Zogg metamorphosed into a local hayseed. His jeans were worn and his plaid shirt soft from washing. He acquired a red hunting jacket and assumed the stoop of a farmer who had spent three-quarters of his life hunching his shoulders against the bite of winter. The stoop, in reality, came from bending over the map tables in the dusty County Planning Office and gazing into his surveying instruments in the field.

He blended into the countryside. He wasn't the sun (which was now perpetually overcast, and growing dimmer and dimmer every day), but he was the grit in the wind, the foreshortened horizon, the red and orange that scorched the fields. He was the fire, like the bruise on Didi's knee, that faded to smoldering browns and yellows with the passing of each evening. After harvest (the combine roaring from dawn to dusk, the crisp sky dusty with debris), he became the mile upon mile of stubble left after the walls of stalks were swept away. He felt in tune with the heartland.

"You comfortable in Addie's bed?" Dusseldorf asked. "Besides not having your own Addie there beside you, uh huh!" Zogg didn't even flinch when Dusseldorf slapped him on the back. "You gotta send out your mating call, Thomas, like a moose does, loud and clear. It's the season."

Zogg wondered how to sound that call. Was it anything like the long, sputtery note Didi blasted on her trombone every morning before the sky turned completely light, to signal to Zogg she was ready to accompany him into the Beaver? Didi summoned him to the hunt. She fixed his midday meal—cornbread, pretzels, apple, dried pork chop sandwiches—and packed it in a gray lunch tin. In return, Zogg carried her trombone to school, switching it from hand to hand at least ten times on the half-mile journey. Didi swung the lunch tin, demolishing the pretzels to crumbs as they rattled inside.

Bit by bit, by teasing it out of her, prodding it forth, by promising Didi a thousand promises he would never live up to (he would take her to the Everglades, Disneyworld, and Cuba, where she could shake for herself Castro's hand), Zogg managed to piece together the story of the young girl in the silver picture frame who haunted him.

Aunt Adeline had been born in Pennsylvania, but came to the Dakotas just before the turn of the century, when her church community decided to escape the influx of foreigners and their evil ways. "My dad says there's nothing worse than a furriner," Didi said, her mouth full of pink chewing gum, "who looks exactly like you but who speaks a language that makes no sense." Adeline grew up a quiet girl— not soft-spoken, but sullen. She spoke German at home, and when she was in town she followed her stern father's instructions never to speak to anyone unless spoken to first. Closed-lipped, her gray eyes downcast, she milked the goats, fed the chickens, and fixed breakfast, lunch, and dinner for her father and seven brothers. Saturday she and her mother did the baking, lump after lump of rye and pumpernickel dough steadily rising in the cast-iron pans.

Adeline tended the crocuses and tulips in the spring. She longed to look after more exotic flowers—roses, gardenias, hyacinths, mums— but her father refused to buy her the seeds, claiming flowers were a luxury. You couldn't feed a family of seven boys on flower petals, and that's what Aunt Adeline was born to have—seven brothers and not a rosebush to her name.

In summer she donned a wide straw hat with a cloth bow beneath her chin and joined her brothers in the field for detasseling. Fall brought harvest, and then the season Adeline hated most—dreary, dreary winter—settled in again. The only thing that kept her happy after a long day of chores was reviewing, by candlelight, her scrapbooks of pressed wildflowers. "Queen Anne's lace," she wrote in her florid hand beneath the specimen. "Daffodil. Black-eyed Susan. Picked by Adeline Hilda Dusseldorf. In such and such a field. On such and such a day. In Shy Beaver, South Dakota, United States of America, North America, the Western Hemisphere, the Earth, the Universe, the Milky Way Galaxy, and whatever there is beyond, year nineteen hundred and seventeen."

Year nineteen hundred and seventeen was the most momentous of Adeline's life. Four of her brothers died on distant fields, but a world war was nothing compared to events on the home front. "It was the year of Jean-François," Didi sighed, as if her breath had been swept away by a sumptuous, colorful picture in a storybook. "Jean-François Milard, the man she adored forever. The man who spelled her ruin."

Zogg heard the low, sweeping sounds of violins. A cymbal crashed. "Tell me," he begged Didi. "Tell me."

Jean-François was a trapper from Canada, a Quebecois, one of the many rough, burly men dressed in leather who passed through Shy Beaver to and from hunting territory. The trappers were heathens, dark-haired, exotic, more beastlike than the animals they set out to capture. By God, if Adeline's father was going to have anything to do with them. "Jean-François—my dad calls him John Francis, or the Frenchie—looked all wrong, dressed all wrong, talked all wrong, smelled all wrong. My dad says the only thing that Frenchie could say in English was *woman,* but that can't be true, else how'd he talk to Aunt Adeline?"

"Love is an animal language," Zogg said.

Didi snorted. "My dad says Aunt Addie couldn't have thought that

Frenchie more romantic if he had sailed in on a gust of perfume and roses from Gay Paree."

Zogg imagined the Eiffel Tower, barges on the Seine, long-skirted women bearing flowers down the Champs-Elysée. "I bet Paris smells wonderful," he said.

"Are you kidding?" Didi held her nose. "With all those French poodles yipping and yapping and turding all over the sidewalk, and with all those smelly cheeses they eat? My dad says there's a whore on every street corner, and what's worse, they don't shave their armpits. I bet the whole country stinks!"

But why were they worrying about France, anyway, when it was a country this Jean-François character had never set eyes upon? He was jaded not by nationality, but by virtue of his age. "He was thirty-two," Didi said, "and by the time you reach that age, you done just about everything. My dad says, 'Yup, Jean-François had met many an Adeline, but Adeline had met only one Jean-François.' You get it?"

Zogg blushed. "Got it."

He came with the other trappers late one winter. Nobody knew how he met Adeline. Maybe she was in her Uncle Diebert's gun shop one day, minding the counter while Diebert slipped across the street to the bar to gulp a shot of whiskey. Then Jean-François stepped in to buy some buckshot, and left the shop with something other than shooting on his mind. Or maybe, just maybe, Adeline delivered a loaf of bread to Diebert's house one afternoon and she walked into a parlor full of trappers, spitting and drinking and cussing. Diebert had Adeline sit down among those furry northern beasts and teach them how to pronounce a few things in English. "Rye bread," Adeline dutifully mouthed for her amused students. "*Teapot. Winchester rifle. Coffee.*" The trappers, whiskey still sticky in their mouths, guffawed and repeated the words in their strange accent: *Hwin-chest-air ree-fell. Caf-fee.* Adeline, accustomed to her aggressive, strapping brothers, still felt awed by the trappers. One in particular—the silent man in the corner who refused to repeat *rye bread* along with the others—had a gaze that penetrated her lace bodice and high collar. Adeline clattered the cups as she served hot tea and fresh bread. She sat primly on her chair, a frog perched on her lily pad, until Uncle Diebert dismissed her with the advice that she not mention the afternoon's activities to her father.

"Hot damn," Didi said, "imagine the look on my Aunt Addie's face when Jean-François showed up in church the next Sunday and sat right down beside her. She probably died. She probably fainted."

"What'd her parents do?"

"Oh, they threatened to lock her in the attic and throw away the key. But then he came a-calling at the house, with fifteen packets of Burpee seeds."

He believed Miss Adeline was fond of flowers? Adeline's father just grunted and turned away. Adeline's mother refused to serve him anything to drink, figuring thirst would send him out of the house and down to the bar that much faster.

"Don't you encourage that beast," her mother hissed, as Adeline gaily sprinkled seeds in the garden.

"Ain't encouraging anybody," Adeline said. "I'm planting flowers."

En garde, Adeline! Zogg silently warned. Beware of Greeks bearing gifts, of the lusty Frenchman come to trap your maiden heart in the jaws of his desire. But it was nature's course. Who could stop a Burpee seed from blooming?

"So then what happened?" Zogg asked. "Did her parents get out a posse and kill him?"

"They just threatened to shoot his face off. That was enough to send him back where he came from."

When he left the Beaver, Adeline mooned like a lovesick cow. She sat beneath the willow behind the Methodist church, scribbling his name with a pencil over and over again on a piece of bark. She wrote him letters which she connived Uncle Diebert into mailing one town over. With the money she had earned from eggs, Adeline took out a post office box. So began a romance by mail.

Héloïse and Abelard, Zogg imagined, had nothing on these newly discovered epistolary lovers. "Let me see the letters," he demanded.

Didi pursed together her lips and shook her head. "Nope. I made a solemn blood vow on Aunt Adeline's deathbed to show them only to the man I married."

"I guess I'm out of luck, then."

"Maybe."

Didi swung the lunch tin, and the pretzels rattled like maracas. "Think I'll be a flamenco dancer when I get to Florida," she said. "Think I'll shake my stuff right on Miami Beach."

But what stuff did she have? If anything, she was growing more caved in and sallow every day. Draped in one of Dusseldorf's old sweaters, she looked tinier and more vulnerable than most of the decapitated mice she regularly whisked out of the traps at Aunt Adeline's. She pinned a posthumous name on each and every rodent that she sent into the netherworld. "This one looks like a Charlie," she yelled out to Zogg. "Here's a Lulu. As my dad would say, a cow just begging for a calf, a 100 percent floozie."

"How can a mouse be a floozie? And what do you know about floozies anyhow?"

"They got red hair and whopper tits. They don't walk, they saunter." Didi threw out her hip, puckered up her mouth, and swirled Lulu the mouse around by its tail. "Play my trombone, big boy."

Zogg took a startled step backwards on the daisy linoleum. "Where'd you learn to talk like that?"

Didi grinned. "You know what my dad does on Friday nights?

Visits the cathouse in Weller. They give him cut-rate 'cause he's sheriff. Aunt Adeline told me, 'Didi, there is nothing more appealing to a certain kind of woman than a man who totes a gun.' They love him."

Zogg's mouth hung open. Slack-jawed, he contemplated that mystery.

The next weekend found him shivering in the cold in Dusseldorf's barn, using the sheriff's .45 to pop pigeons off the rafters.

"Just aim your weapon," Dusseldorf said, "clutch the trigger, and fire. Haw! Got her!" He clapped Zogg on the back as a pigeon, wings half spread, dropped to the ground. Zogg's arm fell slack by his side. The pigeon was dead. He had taken a life! He raced out of the dark and lost his lunch on the side of the barn.

Dusseldorf came up behind him as he retched. "Bad pork chop?"

Zogg shuddered. If he felt that strongly about killing a pigeon, what would happen when he robbed some sweet young thing of her virginity? Would he weep all night long at the violence of it? He straightened up and wiped an icy hand across his mouth. "Give me the gun. I feel like shooting myself."

"It's just a bird, boy." Dusseldorf patted him on the back. He scratched his bald spot. "What are you doing this Friday night?"

"I'm usually tired—"

"Seems to me it'd do you good to accompany me out to Weller."

"Maybe when I feel better."

"You just got indigestion."

"I feel a fever coming on."

"Do you good to sweat," Dusseldorf said.

"Isn't it supposed to snow this weekend?"

"Four-wheel drive, boy. Friday night a date?"

"Friday nights I write to my mother."

"Your mother!" Dusseldorf let out a haw. He squinted. "You in love with somebody?"

With relief, Zogg thought of Pioneer Adeline. "You could say that."

"Well, I'll be. Something Didi said the other night—well, guess that explains it. Come on in and join the family for supper."

So Didi was privy to Zogg's secret fantasies for Adeline. How had she guessed? Maybe Adeline #2 had noticed the dreamy look that overtook his face whenever they talked of her namesake. Maybe she had begun to suspect when he had pressed her repeatedly for details about the Adeline of long ago. Maybe, when she made her daily visit to the mousetraps, she had rooted through the wastebasket and found the sheet of paper he had inscribed in a florid hand, writing *Adeline Hilda Dusseldorf* over and over again. *Thomas Zogg, Esquire, requests the pleasure of your company at his marriage to Miss Adeline Dusseldorf, First Methodist Church, Shy Beaver, South Dakota. Pig on a spit and corn on the cob served immediately after the ceremony. The couple will honeymoon in Cody, Wyoming, on a dude ranch where Mr. Zogg has already proven his prowess as a cowboy. After the honeymoon, Mr. Zogg will ascend into the northern territories to club a few seal. Later this season, the bride will sport a new fur coat, and be voted the best-dressed woman in the Beaver . . .*

Didi stuck her head out the back door. "CHOWTIME!" she hollered.

His secret love discovered, Zogg figured he had nothing to lose by discussing Addie at the dinner table.

"What happened after Jean-François left her?"

"She ice-skated around and around on the pond," Didi said. "She got skinnier and skinnier, skinnier than I am now. She was on the Jean-François diet."

"That cad," Dusseldorf growled. "Damn Canuck in furs."

"Did he jilt her?"

"Jilt her?" Dusseldorf asked. "He was already married, to some Eskimo woman."

Didi smirked. "He put her in the family way."

Zogg was shocked. "Adeline?"

"No, the Eskimo," Dusseldorf said. He attacked his baked potato with his knife and fork. "You'd better believe he married her, too, or they would have harpooned him like a seal."

"They would have gutted him like a walrus, and passed him around as blubber to eat," Didi said. "They would have fed his eyeballs to the dogs. They would have stuffed his intestines like chitlins—"

"Didi, cut that out," Dusseldorf said.

"So when the trappers came down next season and Aunt Adeline found he was stuck in Yellowknife with this Eskimo woman, she threatened to kill herself," Didi continued. "She was going to commit hari-kari. She read all about it in a book."

"Addie's father said good-bye to bad rubbish, but Uncle Diebert, he was all for going up north and shooting that Frenchie right between the eyes like a buck," Dusseldorf said. "Trouble was, he didn't know how to drive a dogsled, and he figured maintaining family honor wasn't worth freezing to death. So he had to settle for cussing this John Francis character out, and Addie had to settle for being a spinster. Most of the Beaver boys died in the war."

"She wouldn't have fallen for any of them anyway," Didi said. "Because she had already fallen for Jean-François, and I mean *fallen*."

"She just made one too many eyes at him, Thomas."

"That's not how I heard it," Didi said. "And I heard it straight from the source."

"Well, the source is dead and gone, so have a little respect. And clear those dishes."

Didi grabbed Dusseldorf's plate and silverware and headed for the wastebasket. As she scraped the bones and gravy into the trash, the fork tines loudly squeaking against the plate, she sang

> *Ain't no use denying*
> *Ain't no use in faking*
> *Eating pig is pretty good*
> *But it can't beat making bacon!*

Dusseldorf shook his head. "She's going to get herself in a heap of trouble someday," he said. "I hope she marries early."

"I hope so, too," Zogg answered, just to be polite.

"Good. Then we're of one mind." Dusseldorf stared at Zogg. "I take my duties as sheriff seriously. I'd hunt down and kill any man who treated my Didi as bad as that Frenchie treated my Aunt Addie."

Zogg nodded sympathetically. Beneath the table, he clutched his knees to suppress his excitement. By God, he'd learn how to shoot a gun if he could accompany the sheriff on such an exciting mission.

"Friday night in Weller still on?" Dusseldorf asked.

To avoid Dusseldorf's gaze, Zogg glanced over at Didi, who was sloppily squirting dishwashing liquid into a sinkful of water.

"Aw, Didi don't care if you're feeling frisky," Dusseldorf said. "That's one thing she's learned from playing that trombone. Practice makes perfect!"

Mr. Thomas Zogg never made it to Weller. He was to make it to bed, the next day, hot and sweaty under the collar, with a temperature of 101 degrees. The change of seasons he had longed to experience ever since he was a boy didn't seem to agree with him. His body recoiled from the world, his toes and fingers curled against the cold, and his teeth constantly chattered. Didi was sent over to nurse him.

"You want an oral or a rectal thermometer?" she shouted from the floral-wallpapered bathroom.

"What do you think?" he asked.

"Rectal's more accurate."

"I'm no stickler for precision."

"Then how'd you get to be a surveyor?" Didi sullenly asked. When Zogg opened his mouth to answer, she stuck the thermometer in. She perched on the edge of the bed and stared at him as he lay there, miserably trying to breathe through his nose and keep his lips shut.

"Guess you won't be going to Weller with my dad after all."

Zogg shook his head.

"Whores carry diseases," she said. "I read all about it in a sex book." She pulled the thermometer out of Zogg's mouth.

"What were you doing reading a sex book?"

"You gotta know those things before you get married, stupid." She squinted at the thermometer. "101 and a half. Whoo-eee. You better get some sleep now, honey."

Zogg crawled back beneath the covers and curled into a ball. Didi fluffed up an extra pillow and stuck it beneath the blankets next to him. "This is called a Dutch Wife," she said. "An extra pillow to hug when the little lady is away. Now you're warm and toasty, just like a little pork chop. Good night, pork chop."

" 'Night," Zogg mumbled.

He fell into a deep slumber. He had the impression Didi hovered about him on the other side of his uneasy sleep, bustling about as he lay there, breathing. But maybe it was the mice rustling in the walls that disturbed his strange dreams.

Zogg slept in bed for one long feverish week. He woke up feeling a little warm and slightly, pleasantly delirious. Didi plied him with burnt toast and Campbell's alphabet soup. "I wiped the mouse turds off the top before I opened the can," she announced as she set the tray down in front of him.

"Thank you."

Didi looked both gratified and sullen. "I hope you don't expect this kind of service from your wife."

Zogg absentmindedly sunk his spoon into the broth and brought up a solitary noodle, the letter *A*. "Why shouldn't I expect it from her?"

"Because she might want to become a marine biologist or something."

"So let her."

"She can't have a career and wait on a man all day."

"Where'd you read that, in your sex book?"

"I read it in *Reader's Digest*, a reliable magazine!" Didi threw the

Shy Beaver Times down on the bed next to Zogg. "You can read the paper if you don't want to conduct a conversation with me. I can tell we don't have an open relationship!"

She stormed out of the room and stomped down the stairs. Zogg stared openmouthed at his alphabet soup. Dusseldorf was right: Didi was loony tunes. The Beaver was in for a shock when she grew up. Zogg shrugged and picked up the *Times*. He slurped his soup as he read the comics; he dropped a *Z* on Charlie Brown's round head and a *D* on Juliet Jones' lush, passionate lips. He turned to the society page for Dear Abby, but instead of Abby he found this:

Bert Dusseldorf, sheriff of Shy Beaver, announces the engagement of his daughter Adeline ("Didi") to Mr. Thomas Zogg, formerly of Miami Beach, Florida.

Zogg roared. "DIDI!" he yelled. "GET UP HERE!"

Complete silence engulfed the house. Zogg swore he heard, in the other room, the snap of yet another mousetrap. Then Didi's flat feet stomped up the stairs. She came in with her hands on her hips.

"Whattaya want now?"

"First of all, take this tray away."

"You can't order me around! We're supposed to be equals now!"

"Take this tray away right now, you little idiot!"

Didi bit her lip. She snatched away the tray and set it on the floor with a clatter.

"What is this?" Zogg yelled, pointing at the newspaper.

"Now it's official. Now everybody knows it. Now I can't say *no* anymore." Fat tears slid down Didi's cheeks. "I wish I never married you!"

"You aren't marrying me. Wait a second." Zogg panicked, remember he had been delirious for a week. "Are we already married?"

"We're getting married in the spring!"

"But I never proposed to you!"

"You wrote my name on scraps of paper and threw 'em in the wastebasket. I found one that said, "Thomas Zogg, Esquire, requests the pleasure of your company—"

"You've been spying on me."

"All's fair in love and war."

"I was talking about Aunt Addie, not you."

"You can't marry Addie. She's dead. Besides, she belonged to Jean-François. He gave her the old plow, twice against the counter in Uncle Diebert's gun shop. She told me. She said it was like a cannonball exploding inside her—"

"Stop it."

Didi stomped her foot. "We were going to honeymoon in Cody, Wyoming. We were going to a dude ranch. I was going to marry you even though you didn't take me to Disneyworld."

Zogg bumbled and stuttered. "I—I—I—"

"I love you." Didi pounced on the bed next to him. Zogg recoiled. He moved over, drawing the Dutch Wife up to his body like armor. "I want to marry you. I want you to make love to me the way those Frenchies do, saying zazaza and zoozoozoo and zeezeezee. Wrestle me like a crocodile. I want to bear your sons. We don't even have to call them Bert, my little Pork Chop, we can call them anything you want—"

Zogg tossed the Dutch Wife aside and leaped out of the bed. In the striped flannel pajamas he had borrowed from Dusseldorf, he took to his bare heels and ran down the stairs. Didi nimbly followed.

"I won't marry you, I won't marry you," Zogg yelled.

"My father'll kill you if you don't!"

Zogg contemplated that for a moment before he continued running. Didi grabbed a broom out of the hall closet and chased after him as if he were a rodent. "If you don't want to marry me, then get out of my house!"

Zogg grabbed the doorknob and opened the door. A biting wind rushed through his bones; wet flecks hit him in the face. It was snowing! Zogg forgot about Didi. He stepped outside, in bare feet and pajamas, and beheld the north as he had truly imagined it—cold, white, and forbidding. A man's world. A man's territory. He was in ecstasy. He held his arms before him as if offering to the sky a sacrificial lamb. He caught snowflakes in the palms of his hand and grew delirious with laughter.

Zogg turned around to go back in. He was going to put on his lumberjack boots and hunting jacket, then go back outside. But the door suddenly, firmly clicked. He tried the doorknob.

Goddang key. Goddang Adeline. The only house in the entire Beaver with a lock on it . . .

"Didi?" Zogg knocked. "Didi? Now Didi, I know you're in there. Didi, it's cold out here." Zogg heard his voice melting into a whine. "Come on, Didi, enough's enough. I'm freezing my . . . Didi, open this door this second!"

Didi's thin, tear-streaked face appeared in the window. She pressed her face flat against the pane and stuck out her long, pink tongue.

"Didi, let me in here!"

With the flat of his hand, Zogg pounded on the door. Didi's face disappeared, and Zogg was left alone, stranded in the wilderness, man against nature, man attacked by a grizzly bear of freezing, devastating snow! He turned away from the house in despair. So this was snow. What was so great about it, anyway? It was just glorified rain. It froze your feet and nipped your cheeks. It bit your ears.

Zogg wandered off the porch. He heard Didi's voice of long ago, saying _You've got to be careful you don't shut yourself out, or you'll freeze yourself solid dead, just like that Injun._ He pondered that for a moment. He considered his options. He could throw himself in the storm cellar, but he didn't have the strength to open it. He could go back and beg Didi's forgiveness, but he didn't have the gumption to marry her. The only other choice was to stand there, fool that he was, in the freezing snow, and stare at the vast heartland that spread before him. This, then, was the cold, cold north. More like the wild, wild west, Zogg thought, wondering where, oh where, was the sheriff when you needed him?